LALO
LESPÉRANCE
NEVER FORGOT

LALO LESPÉRANCE NEVER FORGOT

PHILLIPPE DIEDERICH

DUTTON CHILDREN'S BOOKS

DUTTON CHILDREN'S BOOKS

An imprint of Penguin Random House LLC, New York

First published in the United States of America by Dutton Children's Books,
an imprint of Penguin Random House LLC, 2023

Copyright © 2023 by Phillippe Diederich

Visit us online at PenguinRandomHouse.com.

Library of Congress Cataloging-in-Publication Data is available.

ISBN 9780593354285

1st Printing

Printed in the United States of America

LSCH
Design by Anna Booth
Text set in Adobe Garamond Pro

To frontline workers

LALO
LESPÉRANCE
NEVER FORGOT

1.

Seventeen days after we went into lockdown, we started spying on the man who stole children. It was early April, just after spring break, and the world felt as if it had suddenly stood still. The streets and sidewalks were empty, and an eerie silence had taken over.

It was Vivi's idea to spy on the man who stole children. We were leaning on the railing of the third-floor walkway in front of her apartment, looking at the mysterious motor home that had appeared at the far end of the parking lot.

"Vintage," Vivi said, her voice muffled by her cloth face mask. "Orange stripes on the side, the brown and tan colors. Trust me. It's vintage."

I thought it was just ugly. But Vivi knew what she was talking about. She dressed like that—bell-bottom jeans, jackets with iron-on patches, mismatched Converse high-tops, that kind of thing. It was her way of hiding the fact that she wore clothes from the Goodwill—we all did—but Vivi had this unique fashion sense. She could take any old piece of clothing and improve it, make it funky, which matched her personality.

The motor home sat quietly, separate from everyone and everything. And it never moved. Day after day it sat there like a big ugly box on wheels.

"It's creepy," Vivi said, and crossed her arms, shifted her weight onto one leg so it made her look angry even though she wasn't. "I mean, who would even park there?"

"Well," I said, "it *is* a parking lot."

"No, don't believe it. There has to be more to it than that."

"Maybe they ran out of gas."

"Lalo." She gave me this look like I'd just farted. "Have you ever heard of ghost ships?"

I wasn't sure. Ever since I was little, I'd had a weird amnesia where I couldn't remember things. My memories were like secret notes in bottles floating in the ocean. If I found one, it was usually vague or written in code. I rarely knew what it meant. Sometimes, I couldn't even remember what I did the day before.

I didn't want to sound dumb, so I said, "Yeah sure, the ghost ships."

"Well, that right there," she said, and pointed over the railing, "is a ghost motor home."

I was sure I'd never heard of a ghost motor home. They probably didn't exist. And honestly, I didn't see anything ghostlike about the one in our parking lot. It looked like a regular dilapidated old motor home, kind of reminded me of Doña Chela's taco truck that used to park in the field on the other side of the highway behind our apartment building before we went into lockdown.

Vivi leaned forward and rested her chin on the rail. "We need to find out who lives there."

"Why?"

"Because."

"What if it's abandoned?"

"It's not," she said. "I can tell."

It looked abandoned to me. Someone probably dumped it there because our block was a dump—like a big, giant trash can in North Fort Myers—a place where old cars rested on blocks, sneakers hung from electric wires, and the walls of the buildings were covered with graffiti. But it was also home. The air smelled of garlic, frying oil, and tortillas. Cumbia, ranchera, and salsa music played so loud the speakers rattled, and everyone knew everyone.

"For real, Lalo. Someone's in there for sure." She placed her index finger over her thumb like a cross and kissed it. "I swear. I can feel it. Lo siento en mi corazón."

Vivi did that sometimes, flipped from English to Spanish as if they were one language. Her parents were Mexican. My mom's Mexican. Well, kind of. Her grandfather was from Mexico. But not my father. He's dead.

2.

Our apartment complex was one of those old Florida buildings from the fifties, all concrete block, four stories with a walkway along the front of each floor with a white metal railing where everyone draped their laundry to dry. It had a set of stairs at each end, but the one on the side closest to the street had been blocked for years, so we really only had one set of stairs. One of the few memories I had from when we moved in was Ma saying it looked like a motel, just needed a big pink neon sign flashing out front.

There were four apartments on each floor. We lived on the second floor. Vivi lived above us. That's where we were when we saw my brother in the parking lot. Claudio was seventeen and not someone you'd wanna hang around with, especially when he was with Hugo and Jesse.

I'd already forgotten about the motor home. But when Vivi made up her mind, she stuck to it. My mom would probably say that was an admirable quality, one of those that define good character. I wasn't so sure.

"¡Oye!" Vivi pulled her mask down to her chin and called, "Claudio, hold up."

Claudio stopped and waited for us to catch up. He adjusted his mask, then buried his hands in the pockets of his black hoodie with the skull of the Punisher on the back. Dude never took that thing off.

"You know the guy that lives in the motor home?" Vivi asked.

Claudio looked at me, his eyes half closed as if he were real sleepy. Then he looked at Vivi, then at me. Then at Vivi again.

"She asked you a question," I said.

"I heard her, fool." Claudio was always calling me fool. I don't think he's ever said a sentence to me that didn't end in "fool."

"So?" Vivi said. "Do you, o qué?"

"No. And I don't wanna see his ugly face. Hugo says el cabrón's disfigured, looks like a monster. Besides . . . ," he said, and lowered his voice just enough so that Vivi and I had to lean in to hear him. "Dude's a fugitive. He's wanted."

"What do you mean, wanted?" I said.

"By the *po*-lice, fool."

I knew my brother. I'd known him for eleven years, five months, and nine days. He wasn't someone you could trust, not one hundred percent. Not even fifty or forty-two percent—probably a lot less.

"You're just trying to scare us." My guess was that the guy was a hermit. Although, right now, with Covid, we were all hermits.

"Believe whatchoo want, fool. But if I were you, I'd stay as far away from that motor home as I could. You never know."

"You never know what?"

But that was it. He just made a face that could be interpreted as a warning or, as Vivi said later, a joke. Then he walked away, shoulders slouched, head covered by the black hood.

"Oye," Vivi called after him. She wasn't going to let things hang just like that. "Why'd the cops want him?"

Claudio turned real slow, pulled his mask down, and spelled it out nice and slow: "Crimes. Against. Humanity."

We shared this long, weird silence, Claudio staring at us like he was waiting for each word to sink deep into our souls. Then Vivi laughed. "That's loco, dude."

I had no idea what a crime against humanity was, but it didn't sound good. I had to ask. "Like what kind of crimes?"

Claudio grinned. "He's a robachico."

"¡Mentiroso!" Vivi laughed, and waved him off as he walked away. "First of all, it's *robachicos*, and someone like that wouldn't just park their motor home in our parking lot."

Robachicos: someone who steals children. It's a stupid myth—something Mexican moms tell their children so they'll behave—kind of like el Coco or la Llorona.

"For sure." I adjusted my mask. "Anyone in the building could call the cops, right?"

"Exactly," Vivi said. "We need to find out who lives there."

"What?"

"Claudio's lying. It's our job to find out the truth."

I didn't ask her why it was our job. It wasn't as if someone was paying us. And we weren't superheroes or anything. Even though Vivi and I had known each other for years, we were only hanging out now because of the pandemic. We weren't allowed to leave the building and there was no one else to hang out with. Covid made us friends. Besides, there was nothing else to do during lockdown.

3.

The next morning when I woke up, I couldn't remember what happened the day before. All I got were small moments, most of which didn't make any sense. I did get these weird images of a blue wall, the alley behind our building, and something about a robachicos—an ugly homeless-looking guy carrying a stinky sack full of children he'd stolen from the streets.

After I got dressed, I met Claudio in the kitchen. "Did Ma come home last night?"

He ignored me, poured himself a bowl of Cap'n Crunch, no milk, and ate standing up at the counter.

"That's three days and three nights in a row," I said.

Ma was always at work. She was a nursing assistant at the community clinic. Claudio told me once she does all the heavy lifting. She has to move and bathe and dress and feed the patients, and also clean their rooms and change their bedpans—where they poop—and take their blood pressure and all that. But Vivi, whose mom is also a nursing assistant, said they do way more than that. She said they give the patients a sense of dignity—they're the ones who help them feel human.

Sometimes when Ma came home, we didn't talk. She was under a ton of stress, putting in a million hours at the clinic ever since Covid started. Claudio was always telling me to chill, not to attack her with a bunch of questions the second she walked in the door.

I hated that, Claudio acting as if he was my father. If Ma didn't want me hanging around her when she got home, she'd tell me. She'd say, "Ya, Lalo, let me catch my breath, por favor."

I watched Claudio eat, chomping on the cereal with his mouth open like a dog. "I'm serious," I said, "she said she was going to get me a soldering kit."

"You can't fix the PlayStation, fool."

"You don't know that."

What Claudio didn't know was that I wasn't fixing the Play-Station. I was going to use it to build a memory machine. I had the whole thing planned out. I was going to connect it to my brain and use it to retrieve and record my memories, maybe even project them on the TV.

"Anyway, it's my PlayStation," he said. "If you screw it up more, you're going to have to pay for it."

"I know." I wasn't worried about that. When he bought the PS3 at a garage sale for, like, twenty bucks, he thought he was getting a deal, but the stupid thing never worked. It had been sitting under my bed for years. "So, when's Ma coming home?"

"Today," he said, and put on his hoodie. "So you better clean the bathroom before she gets here." Then he stomped away.

Claudio didn't have to tell me. I always did my chores. Always. I had them listed on a piece of paper on the wall by my bed so I wouldn't forget. The ones in red were my daily chores, like making my bed and showering and stuff, and the ones in blue were my weekly chores, like cleaning the bathroom, doing my laundry, and all that.

Still, I wrote a daily note on my hand so I wouldn't forget—just in case. That was my thing. I'd been doing it since the third grade when I asked Coach Díaz about the tattoo of a mean-looking pitchfork he had on his forearm. I thought it had something to do with the devil, but he said it was to remind him of his grandfather who had been a farmer in Cuba. I figured I could do that, too, write stuff on my hand to remember things I liked, like maduros and guarapo and important stuff from class and what I had to do at home and the names of kids who'd been mean to me.

I grabbed my backpack and followed Claudio out of the apartment. "At what time?"

He didn't answer, just walked up the stairs with his head slouched, staring at his phone like a zombie.

When we went into lockdown and school went virtual, Claudio and I had to go to class at Vivi's apartment because we didn't have internet at our place. Ma said she forgot to pay the bill and the cable company was demanding a huge deposit to reconnect us. When Claudio told her maybe she should just pay it, she went loca. "Never. I'm not falling for that." Then she called them racists, thieves, sinvergüenzas, and a bunch of other fine words we're not supposed to say.

Later, Claudio told me Ma was lying about the internet, that it was just a convenient excuse because she didn't want us to be alone in the house when we were supposed to be in school. "Ma ain't no dummy, fool," he'd said, and slapped me on the back of the head. "She knows if we stay home by ourselves, we'll just watch TV and sleep all day."

I didn't trust Claudio, but he was probably right because that was pretty much what we did after school before lockdown.

4.

When Claudio and I got to Vivi's apartment, he put his mask on, pumped out a squirt of hand sanitizer from the bottle on the dining room table, and parked himself at the kitchen counter, where he took his classes on his phone. Vivi and I were in sixth grade, so we sat together at the dining room table with a laptop we got from school. We actually got two laptops—one for her and one for me—but mine broke the first week of virtual school and they hadn't replaced it yet. Which was fine. It was more fun like this. It felt as if we were in school together. Vivi's older sister, Lupe, was a sophomore. She stayed in the bedroom she shared with Vivi, never came out.

Their apartment was exactly like ours. One bedroom for Lupe and Vivi and one for their mom and grandmother, with a bathroom between the two rooms. Even the kitchen was in the same place, with the same brown counter and white cabinets. The only difference was that they had their living room set up different from ours. We had the couch with its back to the big window that faced the front walkway. They had theirs against the side wall just past the front door. That's where Alita always sat, unless she was at her sewing machine by the big front window.

Vivi's mom was a nursing assistant like my mom, but she worked at the big hospital downtown. Vivi told me she was living at a motel near the hospital with someone she worked with because she didn't want to risk bringing Covid home and infecting anyone. She only came back like once a week for dinner and to do laundry. So Alita took care of Vivi and Lupe and watched all of us during school. She was from Mexico and spoke English with a real heavy accent. Alita is short for "abuelita," but it's funny because it's also what Ma calls chicken wings—alitas—"small wings." She bakes them in the oven with salt and chile piquín until they're brown and crispy and a little spicy.

I never met my grandparents, so I liked to imagine Alita was also my grandmother. She was tiny and real thin. She had long gray hair she braided at the back and that went down to her waist. My favorite thing about going to school online at Vivi's was Alita, because she told us all kinds of cool stories about Mexico and Mexican magic and stuff.

Vivi logged us into Zoom. "So?"

I pumped a little sanitizer onto my hands and rubbed them together. "So what?"

She set her pen down. "So, after school, no?"

I smelled the palms of my hands.

"Why do you always have to do that?"

"I like it," I said, and smelled my hands again. "It smells like a Sharpie."

"Robachico." She turned the volume down on the computer, where the teacher had just started talking. "Don't tell me you don't remember."

"Kind of." I hated forgetting. It made me sound dumb. I looked at my hand to see if I'd written something to remind me, but there were only two words, *clean bathroom.*

Vivi rolled her eyes and explained everything that happened in the last couple of days, about the motor home and our deal to find out about Robachico.

It sounded sketchy to me. "Why don't we just ask Alita to—"

"No!" Vivi barked. "We can't. She'll just tell us not to go near it."

"Then maybe we shouldn't."

"Dude. You're not chickening out?"

"No . . ." I glanced across the hall. "What about Lupe? Maybe we should include her." Lupe was always alone, even before Covid. "She never comes out."

"So?"

"I don't know." I felt bad for Lupe because she sort of had this sad, angry air about her. "Maybe she'd like to hang out with us."

"She wouldn't," Vivi said. "She doesn't like people."

But it was more than that. Lupe never talked, even when we were little. It was as if she was angry all the time, never smiled or anything. Her favorite color was black—like, black everything: clothes, hair, lipstick. Even her bedroom door was painted black and covered with stickers.

"We can just ask her," I said.

"No way." She gave me this look, her thick eyebrows pressing down over her eyes. "She'll just complain about everything and ruin the whole thing. Besides, I don't want Lupe up in my business. Period."

"Yeah, but—"

"*Lalo*. She's my sister. I love her and all, but I know her too well. She's weird with a capital *W*."

"Vivi—"

"¡Ya!" She raised the palm of her hand to my face. She did that. Stopped you like a cop. "I'm not having this conversation."

Before Covid, I was alone even though I was surrounded by a bunch of other kids at school. Now that we were in lockdown, I wasn't alone. And they skipped my accommodations, too. Before Covid, I got special help because they said my memory problem was a learning disability—kind of like ADHD. So I got extra time for tests and had special tutoring on Fridays. Now Vivi and I shared a computer. We took the same virtual classes and no one said anything about my accommodations or gave me extra time or anything. And I didn't ask. Even before we started using Zoom for school and were using Teams and it became this huge problem for everyone, I never asked for help. It was cool to be normal for a change.

My biggest problem with school was reading. It always felt as if I hadn't read anything even though I had. And sometimes, I'd be in class and then forget whatever the teacher said. I don't mean little parts. I mean the whole thing. It was as if I hadn't even been there.

I never knew what I was going to forget and what I was going to remember. Like when I was little and got sick with asthma. It lasted for years. Ma had to give me medicine from an inhaler using a plastic spacer. I remember everything. The spacer had these little pictures of a brown-and-yellow cartoon bear. Ma would say, "Lalo, it's puff-puff time!"

I'd sit on her lap and she'd place the part that was like an oxygen mask over my mouth and nose and put the inhaler on the other end of the tube and we'd sing, "Puff-puff . . . it's puff-puff, la-la-la." We were real happy and cheerful about it as if she was giving me a treat. The spray from the inhaler smelled like cinnamon and the stuff she used to clean the bathroom. I'd breathe it in while she checked her Mickey Mouse watch. I would count the pictures of the happy bear on the tube. I remember that as if it happened yesterday. Ma's hair was long and loose back then, and she wore these big red-and-blue earrings in the shape of Haiti—shaped like a claw. Now, whenever I count, I think of Ma and the two of us singing the puff-puff song and the smiling bear.

But there's a ton of stuff I can't remember. Like, I can't remember moving into our apartment or my first day of middle school, which happened only eight months ago, or the place where we lived before here, or a bunch of stuff from elementary school. I can't even remember my father.

The way I explained it to the doctor was that it was as if there were holes in my brain. Like, say my memories were a slice of cheese. In the places where there's cheese, I remembered. But there's a bunch of holes in the cheese. In those holes there's nothing.

5.

When I came home from Vivi's after school, Ma was in her bedroom, resting. I checked my hand. Two notes—the one about cleaning the bathroom, and a new one: *Spy on Robachico's motor home.* I sat by the window and kept an eye on the motor home with binoculars. They weren't real, just a plastic toy that made things a tiny bit closer. You couldn't even focus them. I got them for Christmas three years ago when the school donated presents for us. Ma cried when we got them. I didn't know if she was happy or sad or what. But we got a trash bag full of wrapped gifts from people we didn't know. We had Christmas. Someone had even donated a ham. We ate leftovers until Cinco de Mayo.

I turned the binoculars to the street. The whole block was deserted except for a couple of homeless guys making their way past the Circle K. They walked real slow, heads bowed, no masks. I followed them until they crossed the street and disappeared around the next corner.

I turned and scanned our living room, paused on the picture of Papi in the gold frame that sat on top of the TV. He looked young, dark brown shiny skin, kinky hair like mine but a lot tighter. He wore it real short with a perfect line on the side. His big brown eyes stared at the camera as if he were trying to see past it. He had a huge smile like a clown.

Papi's name was Claude—Claude Lespérance. He was Haitian. Claudio was named after him because he was born first. But he told everyone to call him Claudio. I was named after Ma's father, Eduardo. But Ma said I was the one who was more like Papi, which was true. Claudio looked Mexican like Ma. I looked black without really being Black—Haitian without being Haitian. I knew nothing about Haiti. I'd never been. Haiti belonged to Papi. Now Haiti didn't exist.

I washed my hands real good, then went into Ma's room. She was awake but lying on her side with her eyes closed. "Ma?"

"What is it?" Her tone was soft and drowsy.

"Did you get the soldering kit?"

"We're on lockdown, Lalo. Nothing's open."

"You can order it from Amazon," I said. "I need it for the memory machine."

"We'll see." She took a deep breath. Her lips made a gentle curve across her face.

"Ma?" I said after a moment. "Did you have robachicos when you were growing up?"

"Did we have them?" She chuckled. "I never saw one, but your grandmother always warned us about el robachicos. And el Coco."

"What about Papi?"

She opened her eyes and turned to face me. "What about him?"

"Do they have robachicos in Haiti?"

Her eyes searched my face for a moment. "They call them loups-garous."

I said it out loud to myself, "Loo-ga-oo . . ."

"They're supposed to be half man and half wolf and only come out on full moons."

"Are they real?"

"I don't know. I've never been to Haiti."

"Did Papi tell you about them?"

She nodded and closed her eyes. "Can we talk about this later?"

I went back to the living room and aimed the binoculars at the motor home. If I caught a glimpse of Robachico, even if he just peeked through a window or snuck his head out the door for a second, Vivi would be so jealous.

A car with the Papa Rico's Pizza sign on the roof turned the corner and parked in front of our building where Socrates was working on a car.

"Ma!" I called. "We getting pizza?"

"Mac and cheese," she said. "Please, Lalo. Let me get some rest."

Before Covid, Ma's job made her happy. She talked to the patients, kept them company, and made sure they were comfortable and stuff. But since Covid hit, she had to do the work of three people all the time because they had so many sick people in the clinic. Everyone had to wear super-protective gear, like N95 masks and face shields. She had to check on patients, turn them, help them go to the bathroom, make sure they were getting their medicine and oxygen. But she said the worst part was helping them on video calls with their families because no one was allowed to visit the clinic. When they said goodbye, you didn't know if it was for the last time.

We wouldn't see Ma for days at a time. When she came home, she had me massage cream on her face where the mask left red lines on her skin. She'd lie on her bed in shorts and a T-shirt, the ceiling fan turned on as fast as it would go. "Lalo, mi amor," she'd call. "Cream, por favor!"

I sat on the bed and massaged the cream onto her face. I loved how her skin felt, smooth and familiar like my own. I could tell it was her even with my eyes closed. My fingers traced the lines of the mask over her nose and down her cheeks and chin. I felt the little pimples on her nose, the beauty mark on the lower part of her right cheek, the scar at the tip of her chin.

Sometimes, when I ran my index finger along the lines of her dented skin, I imagined it was a racetrack and my fingers were cars. They went around and around the dips and curves of her face.

Ma kept her eyes closed when I massaged her face. Sometimes she'd ask me about my day. But she had this thing about being careful with her questions. Sometimes, when I couldn't remember something, I got upset. Not with her, just in general. I got so frustrated. So she's extra gentle with me, which annoyed me. I hated being treated special, like I'm fragile or something. It made me feel dumb.

When I massaged Ma's face, her lips stretched, and her cheeks dimpled when she smiled. She had two big front teeth. One was a bit crooked. I loved that. Nobody else in the world had a smile like hers.

In five minutes, she'd be asleep.

She looked serious like that—sleeping. Maybe she dreamed of work or of Covid. Or of something that upset her. Like Claudio.

Ma worried about all kinds of things. But she never talked about them. She just did things—went to work, came back, made dinner, gave orders, cleaned the apartment, did laundry, told us what to do, what not to do. She didn't waste time because she didn't have any to waste.

Claudio and I had too much time.

6.

The next morning when we got to Vivi's, Alita served us hot chocolate—except for Claudio. His ritual was to nuke himself a cup of water, add two spoonfuls of Nescafé, two of sugar, and a dab of milk for a café con leche. But Alita's hot chocolate was the best. She got it from the Mexican market and frothed it with a molinillo, this wooden whisk contraption she turned with her hands. It made the chocolate real light and airy so it felt as if you were drinking a cloud of sugar and chocolate.

Vivi sat at the dining room table in front of the laptop with her mask hanging under her chin, a thick chocolate mustache on her upper lip.

I pointed at her face. "Nice."

"My name is Don Frank," she said in a deep, manly voice. "Would you like a paleta, niño?"

Don Frank was one of our neighbors. His real name was Francisco, but everyone called him Don Frank. He lived on the first floor. His door was the first one by the stairs, then next was Socrates's apartment, then Irma's, and then the one where

Nazario, the property manager, lived with his wife, Sandra, and their son, Hugo. Don Frank was Alita's friend. They came from the same town in Mexico. He always dressed like a cowboy— jeans, boots, and a nice white Western hat. He sold ice cream from a bike with a cooler in the front. Every morning he'd go to la Michoacana and fill the cooler with paletas and frozen treats, then he'd ride around the neighborhood ringing his little bell to let everyone know he was there. Sometimes, in the evenings, he'd bring us leftover paletas—for free.

I lowered my mask and took a sip of my chocolate, got my own mustache. We laughed hysterically.

"A ver, niños." Alita clapped her hands like a teacher. "Las máscaras, por favor."

"We're drinking." Vivi took another sip of chocolate.

I put my mask back on.

"You see this design?" Alita ran her index finger across her mask. It had a red-and-pink embroidery in the shape of a bird. "It's an ancient Olmec symbol from Veracruz."

"I like it," I said.

Alita made her own masks and spent hours embroidering Mexican designs on them before taking the bus all the way to the Guadalupe Center in Immokalee, where they gave them away to the poor.

"Tiene poderes mágicos," she said. "The person who wears it is protected against evil."

"Alita, we're not little kids," Vivi said. "There's no such thing as magic powers."

"Sí, eres muy lista, Viviana—you're very smart. But you

should open your mind, mija. México tiene muchísimos secretos. You need to learn about our customs. If you allow the spirits of your ancestors into your heart, you'll be surprised to find magic in the most unlikely places."

I believed in Mexican magic—totally. I didn't know whether her mask had powers or not, but I believed what Alita told us. A lot of things happen that have no explanations, like the crop circles and the image of the man in a spaceship carved in a Mayan pyramid, Bigfoot, the Bermuda Triangle. And the Aztec calendar. But even if there wasn't any magic, her stories took me far away. From the way she talked, it made me wish I lived in the old days in Mexico. Back then, there was magic everywhere.

"That Covid will never get me," Alita said, and made her way back to her sewing machine. "Ya verán."

Vivi put her mask on and whispered, "My mask has special powers, too. It protects me against broccoli, mayonnaise, and liver."

"What about garlic?" I said.

"No way. I love garlic."

I laughed. "Me too."

We opened our history books. The teacher started talking about the Emancipation Proclamation.

"¿Entonces?" Vivi said after a moment.

"What?"

"Did you see Robachico, o qué?"

I shook my head. "I'm fixing the PS3. I'm going to invent—"

"Lalo—"

"I'm serious," I said. "As soon as my mom gets me the

soldering kit, I'm going to make a machine that will help me remember everything that has happened in my life."

"So, like a time machine."

"No, a memory machine."

"If it's going to remind you of what happened," she said, "wouldn't it take you back in time to see what happened?"

I hadn't thought of that. I just figured the machine would take memories from my brain and store them so I could see them on a TV, like in a video game. But maybe Vivi was right.

"I'll know for sure once I start putting the machine together," I said. "Maybe it'll do both things."

"Okay, but what about Robachico? We have to keep spying on him."

"Did you even look?"

"A little. But you-know-who"—she nodded toward Alita—"is always watching me."

"Just look out the window. That's what I did."

"You have binoculars."

"They don't really work."

"But they're better than nothing," she said, and pulled her long black hair over her shoulder and started braiding it.

"What if the motor home's abandoned?"

"It can't be."

"There's never any lights on or anything."

"Duh, it has curtains? Curtains block out the light?"

"You don't have to say it like that." I hated when people made it sound like I was stupid.

"I'm just saying."

"Why don't we just go and knock on the door?" I said.

"Dude, if he's a real robachicos or a criminal or whatever? Then what?"

"Don't believe Claudio," I said. "He's full of it."

"Full of what?"

I glanced at Alita leaning over her sewing machine, then spelled it out for Vivi: "Ca-ca."

7.

After lunch, Alita usually sat on the couch, where she embroidered designs on the masks using a needle and colored threads. But now she just sat there like a statue, tiny and sad. Her eyes seemed lost in the space in front of the bureau that had a bunch of family photos, a couple candles, and a framed image of the Virgen de Guadalupe.

I nudged Vivi. "Alita looks sad."

"She does that. My amá says it's nostalgia."

"What's that?"

"It's like when you remember things with your heart."

"You can do that?"

"When you're old," she said, and turned the page of her math book.

"Maybe she wants to go back to Mexico."

"It's not just Mexico. It's her youth."

"Maybe I've been doing it all wrong," I said, "and that's why I can't remember."

"No. Es cosa de viejitos. You have to be old."

It didn't make sense. Even when you're a kid you have a heart. Like, in the present when things are happening, I could feel it in my heart. I didn't see why I couldn't remember stuff with my heart. Especially something that really mattered—like my father.

Alita whispered something and nodded. I glanced at Vivi, but she was glued to the computer, where the teacher was saying something about isosceles triangles and how they have two equal sides and all that.

For a moment I thought Alita was praying, but then she smiled. People don't smile when they pray. Then she said something about a butterfly. "I told it my wish," she said with a nod. "That's how it happened. El resto es historia."

"Alita?" I said. "You okay?"

She turned to me and nodded. "I'm talking to José Antonio." Then she looked ahead and said something about the monarch butterflies that filled the garden of their house in Cuajimalpa with so much color in the spring.

I turned to Vivi. "Who's José Antonio?"

"My abuelo," she said without turning away from the computer. "He died before I was born."

"She's talking to him?"

"To his spirit," she said with a shrug. "Apparently, he comes and goes whenever he wants."

"For real?"

Vivi winced and touched the side of her head with her index finger. "She's a little, you know, loquita."

I wasn't so sure. The way she sat there, staring at the space between her and the bureau, it was as if someone was really there. I focused on the same place as Alita. She was talking about the goddess of happiness and flowers, and about Covid and the lockdown and that José was lucky he wasn't here to suffer through it. I couldn't understand all of it because it was in Spanish, but her tone was soft and tender. I could tell she loved him very much, even in spirit. And as I stared at the empty space between Alita and the bureau with all the photos, it felt as if José was really there. I couldn't see him or anything, but I got a light smell, like vanilla and tobacco. His presence had to be real, like Robachico. He was there but not there at the same time.

Then a man's tinny voice said, "Mi amor."

I blinked and glanced at Vivi. "Did you hear that?"

"Yeah." She nodded at the laptop. "Mr. Jinich asked you a question."

Our math teacher was staring at me, his unshaven face filling the computer screen. "For the last time, the difference between an isosceles and an equilateral triangle, Lalo?"

8.

I promised Vivi I would spy on Robachico, but when I left her apartment after school, I went home to work on the PS3.

Before we went into the lockdown, I had started drawing out my idea in one of my notebooks. The plan was to run three wires from the motherboard of the machine to the parts of my brain where memories are stored. One electrode would access the hippocampus, which is the part of the brain that catalogues memories. My science teacher, Mr. Z, said this was one of the most important parts of the brain as far as memories are concerned. The second electrode was going to be connected to the amygdala, which is where emotional memories are kept. For me this was the most important part because my goal was to retrieve memories of my father. The third electrode was going to connect to my prefrontal cortex, which deals with short-term and immediate memories.

I was going to connect the wires from the PS3 to my brain using Band-Aids as electrodes. When I turned on the PS3, the electrodes would retrieve my memories the same way the PS3 retrieves information from a video game disk and records them to the hard drive. If my calculations were correct, I could connect the console to the TV and it would play the memories while recording them. When I showed my design to Mr. Z, he was impressed. He said it was a very detailed schematic and had real possibilities, and that I should consider entering the project in the science fair. When I got home that day, I looked up the word *schematic*—it's science talk for a detailed diagram.

My biggest problem was that Claudio had pretty much destroyed the PS3 when he tried to fix it. He tore the cover off, so that was gone. Also, the wires to connect the hard drive were missing and the CD drive was in pieces. I didn't think the CD drive was repairable—at least not by me. That didn't matter since I wasn't going to use it. But there were a bunch of small pieces lying around that I didn't know where they went. I didn't want to lose them, so I started taping them to a piece of white poster board and labeling them so I wouldn't forget. Once Ma got me the soldering kit, I was going to put it all together as a memory machine.

When I finished taping the last of the small pieces to the poster board, I placed it neatly on top of my dresser. I grabbed the binoculars and went to the living room to spy on Robachico's motor home. The parking lot was deserted, except for Don Frank. He was leaning over his bike cooler. Irma's little kids, Beto and Eric, were standing there, six feet away, staring at him.

I ran downstairs.

Don Frank pushed his hat up over his brow when he saw me coming. He was sweating. And he wasn't wearing a mask. "No tengo nada," he said, then looked at the kids who were staring at him like a pair of starving little zombies, a dollar bill in each of their hands. "I'm telling you, pues. No hay paletas, niños. I'm only cleaning the bike. Go on and play."

The kids looked at me. Beto, who was the older one, grabbed Eric's hand and pulled him away.

Don Frank nodded at the binoculars in my hand. "What's with them?"

I looked at the binoculars, at the motor home. "Just playing," I said. "What are you doing?"

"El lockdown." He set the rag he was holding on top of the cooler and took a deep breath. "La Michoacana's closed. I got no product to sell. It's tough, amigo. Quizá—I don't know—I might have to sell the bike. Pero entonces, qué? What do I do then?"

I didn't know what to say. But maybe the question wasn't really for me because he went on talking, his eyes focusing past me at the apartment building and the highway overpass—and even farther to the field or, who knows, maybe Mexico, like Alita always did.

"They say the government's going to freeze rents and give us a little help," he went on. "Pero como no tengo papeles, I doubt I'll see any of that. And ese Nazario, you know how he is. You think he'll give anyone a break on the rent?" He shook his head and chuckled softly.

I knew the answer to his question. Ma always complained about Nazario. It was almost impossible to get him to fix anything because he was too busy with what she called his "side hustles," but when it was time for the rent, he acted as if he owned the building and was doing us a favor by letting us live in it.

"Yo ya no sé," Don Frank said, and started wiping down his bike. "I don't know what I'm gonna do."

"I'm sorry," I said.

"¿Qué se va hacer? That's life, no?"

He kept wiping the bike, but it was already super clean. The chrome was shiny, and the cooler was bright white with a painting of a made-up cartoon character that looked a little like a cowboy Mickey Mouse on the sides and the words HELADOS DON FRANK written in fancy cursive.

I felt weird just standing there, not doing anything, so it came out of me without thinking: "Do you know who lives in that motor home?"

He turned his head and glanced at the back of the parking lot for a second. "Quién sabe. Irma said she thought it was an old gabacho who comes out only at night. The way things are going around here with the Covid and all that, I wouldn't be surprised if he's la Santa Muerte—the Grim Reaper. No faltaba más. My advice is to stay clear of it."

9.

The next day after class, Alita called us to the couch. "Vengan, pues, niños."

Vivi looked at me and whispered, "Don't go." Her brow furrowed with worry. "We have to spy on Robachico."

"Ándale, Viviana." Alita tapped the seat beside her. "You too, Lalo. Come on. Let's learn Spanish."

I closed the laptop and went to the couch.

"I can't." Vivi gathered her books. "I need Lupe's help with my science homework." And before Alita could say anything, she rushed to the bedroom.

I didn't mind being with Alita. I sat next to her and slowly felt myself leaning into her, my cheek against her shoulder. She smelled like rain and the quesadillas she'd made us for lunch. Even the sound of her voice was special, like a song. Every muscle in my body relaxed, made me feel like I was floating. It made me think of her husband and whether he felt this way, as if the air were thick and tasted of salt.

She had me repeat a few phrases in Spanish, then placed her

hand on my knee. "You have to practice, Lalo. If you don't, you will never learn Spanish."

"I know. But I forget and Ma doesn't talk to us in Spanish." That wasn't one hundred percent true. Ma spoke English with little bits of Spanish, like Vivi. She wasn't very Mexican. She's never even been there, and she never talked about Mexico or Mexican magic.

"Maybe you should watch a few telenovelas with me," Alita said. "I was just talking with my old friend Rosita Villalobos. She learned English from watching American movies."

"Was she here?" I said that because Alita had been sitting on the couch all day, except when she was in kitchen cooking lunch. I didn't remember anyone coming to the door. I was pretty sure. But then again, maybe I forgot.

"Claro. She was here. And José Antonio, too. We talk all the time," she said, and tapped my knee with the tips of her fingers. She glanced across the room at her wedding photo on the bureau. She was young, looked just like Lupe but without all the black makeup. And José was real serious, with long sideburns and a thick black mustache like a bandido in an old cowboy movie.

"What did you talk about?" I said.

"Well, I was remembering the time I made a wish that came true."

"For real?"

"Claro. If you whisper your wish to a butterfly, it becomes true. It's a Náhuatl legend. But it's true. I know this because it happened to me."

"What did you wish for?"

She smiled and stared ahead at the empty space in front of the bureau. "I wished José Antonio would fall in love with me."

"Butterflies used to give me the creeps," I said. "But not anymore."

"Pero, mijo, they're beautiful creatures. The monarch butterfly in particular has a very special place in the hearts of the Mexican people."

"But they're caterpillars, and then they sprout wings," I said. "You don't think that's weird?"

"No, no. It's a miracle," she said. "Butterflies are precious. It's moths you need to be wary of."

"Moths give you the creeps?"

"No, ¿cómo crees?" She waved. "But a black moth coming into your house at night is a terrible omen." She leaned closer to me and whispered, "It means someone is going to die."

"For real?"

She nodded and stared at the pictures on the mantel.

"Are they poisonous?"

"Eh?"

"The moths," I said. "Why do people die when it comes into the house?"

"The moth is a messenger," she said matter-of-factly. "It's just one of those things. Everyone knows that."

This didn't make sense, but most of Alita's stories didn't make sense, like the voladores. She said there were men in Papantla, in the state of Veracruz, who had the power to fly. When I asked her where they went, she said they flew in circles to make it rain so their crops would grow. What was the point of that? If I could fly, I'd visit faraway places like Africa or the Amazon.

Alita stared, eyes big and shiny as she seemed to get lost in the pictures of her past.

"Are you homesick?" I asked.

"No, how could I be?" she said. "This is my home."

"I mean for Mexico."

She took my hand and led me to the bureau. We studied the photos of her wedding, of Vivi and Lupe when they were little, and a bunch of other ones of Vivi's parents and all their family in Mexico.

"Everyone I love is here," she said.

They were a huge family, so many different people in the pictures and everyone smiling and happy except for José Antonio, who always looked serious. At home we only had pictures of Ma and Papi, Claudio and me.

"I hope we never have to go back to regular school," I said.

"Pero why would you say such a thing, mijo?"

"So I can keep coming here and be with you and Vivi."

"No, you do not mean that," she said. "Don't you miss your friends?"

I didn't tell her that she and Vivi were my only friends.

10.

Later that day, I went up to the roof to meet Vivi and spy on
Robachico. To get to the roof, you had to go up to the fourth
floor and climb up a secret set of stairs on the far side of the
building. But they weren't really secret. They were just not part
of the regular stairs. You went through a door that didn't have a
handle and up this narrow hallway. But when you walked out on
the roof it was as if you were walking onto a football field, long
and flat and empty, except instead of grass there was concrete
and gravel.

You could see everything from there: the parking lot in the
front; the street; the Circle K; the alley in the back; and past it,
the highway overpass and part of the empty lot on the other side
of it. And there was always a breeze, made it feel as if you were
moving with the building.

I sat on the edge of the roof facing the front and looked out
on the parking lot. I almost didn't recognize our block. It was
deserted. Not even a stray dog, just a couple of vultures cir-
cling up in the clouds. And the silence—no music, no cars, no

laughter. It was so quiet, I could even hear the palm trees on the next block rustling in the breeze.

A little while later, Vivi showed up wearing a blue mask with bright pink and green flowers.

"New mask?" I said.

"Alita made it for me."

"Is it magic?"

She rolled her eyes and sat. "You really believe her stories?"

"Kind of. I mean, why not?"

"'Cause they're not real."

"You don't know that," I said. "Not everything that happens can be explained with logic."

"Science," she said, her head raised as if she were declaring something super important. "I believe in science."

"But you believe in robachicos."

"Yeah." She grabbed the binoculars from me and looked at the motor home. "But that has nothing to do with magic."

"It kind of does," I said. "Think about it. What you—"

"Ya." She raised the palm of her hand to stop me. "I don't want to get into that right now." Then she handed me the binoculars. "Nada."

"I'm telling you. It's abandoned . . . except Don Frank . . ."

"Don Frank what?"

A door slammed shut on the floor below us. "Pero Dios mío," a woman said, "¿y ahora qué?"

"It's Altagracia," Vivi whispered.

"Dime, Osvaldo, what are we gonna do now, eh?" Altagracia's voice was shaky. She was Dominican from over there, spoke with a real thick accent. She wore colorful bandanas over her hair and had this graceful way of gesturing with her arms when she spoke. She was always nice to me, but Ma didn't like her because she said Altagracia didn't like Haitians.

"It's not just me, mi amor," Osvaldo said. "It's half the staff." Osvaldo was Altagracia's husband. He was Cuban like Socrates but had dark skin like mine.

"They should keep you," Altagracia cried.

"No te preocupes. We'll figure something out." Osvaldo's tone was tense. His words tightened at the end as if he didn't want to let go of them.

"What about the rent next month, eh?" Altagracia said sharply. "How we gonna eat, y pañales pa'l baby?"

"I'll find other work."

"Four years, Osvaldo. You gave them four years. And this is how they treat you?"

"Business is dead, mi amor. They can't keep everyone on."

"I don't care about everyone else," Altagracia cried. "They should keep you."

"He lost his job," Vivi whispered.

I nodded. In our building, everyone worried about money—even before Covid. Ma complained about it. Socrates fixed cars to make extra cash, Don Frank sold ice creams and paletas, and Nazario was always working on some crazy scheme, like the time he bought a storage container full of stuff. He had a yard sale every weekend for two months and still couldn't get rid of all the junk.

Listening to Osvaldo and Altagracia made Alita's Mexican stories about spirits and magic seem unreal—like cartoons.

"Oye." Vivi nudged me. "Don Frank what?"

"What about him?"

"We were talking about Robachico," Vivi said. "You said the motor home was abandoned, except Don Frank . . ."

"Except Don Frank what?"

"That's what I'm asking," she said with a frown. "What were you going to say?"

I stared at her for a second, glanced over at the motor home, and back at her. But I couldn't remember. "I don't know," I said, and held the binoculars out for her.

She raised them to her face and focused on the motor home for a long time. "This weekend is supposed to be Jessica Weston's birthday party," Vivi said real casual. "You know her?"

"I know who she is." Jessica was one of the popular girls at school. She didn't talk to me—didn't even see me.

"She's like my best friend."

"You gonna go?"

"Dude." She put down the binoculars and gave me this look. "We're on lockdown."

"I know."

"It was going to be a dance party."

"And your mom was okay with that?"

She rolled her eyes and turned away. "I miss my friends. Stupid Covid."

"My mom says it's not forever."

"I know. But meanwhile, I'm stuck here with Alita and you and Robachico."

"Why do you say that?"

"'Cause it's true."

"Yeah, but we're friends, no?"

She stared at me for a second, then turned to face the parking lot. "Yeah, because there's no one else."

"That's mean." I took the binoculars from her. "I thought you liked hanging out."

"Dude," she said, and grabbed my wrist, "I'm just being honest. We never hung out before. We don't have the same friends."

"I hate those guys, anyway," I said, thinking of Jessica and Tommy Maldonado and Brittany whatever-her-last-name-was. Those guys didn't even know I was alive. "I don't know why you even hang out with them."

"You don't know them," she said angrily.

"What about us?"

"We're on stakeout," she said, took the binoculars from me, and checked out the motor home.

"But we're friends, right?"

She glanced at me over the binoculars, but I couldn't tell whether she was smiling or not because of the mask. "Just don't dis my friends, okay?"

She looked out at the parking lot for what felt like forever. The sun was burning down on us. It was getting really hot. I wanted to go inside, but I wanted to stay, too. I wondered if we'd hang out when lockdown ended. Probably not. Vivi was right. We were neighbors and went to the same school, but we lived in different worlds.

"Maybe we should just go knock on his door," I said.

She put down the binoculars and sighed.

"What's the big deal?" I said.

"That he might grab us and kidnap us or something."

"Dude, Claudio's lying."

"What if he's not?"

There was always a chance. A part of me liked sitting on the roof with Vivi, but there was that other part—the one that felt empty. She was right. We were not real friends. It was all because of Covid and the lockdown. Maybe that's why I said it. "You dare me, or what?"

Vivi stared at me, her eyes narrow. "To go knock?"

I squinted at the motor home as if I were measuring the distance from here to there and nodded.

Vivi laughed. "Estás loco, Lalo. Really."

"No, no," I said because she was so excited and it was too late to back out. "I'll do it. For real."

11.

The next morning when I got to Vivi's for school, she reminded me that I'd chickened out. I'd forgotten all about the dare and that we'd been on the roof spying on Robachico and even that Altagracia had been crying about Osvaldo losing his job at the restaurant.

Vivi rolled her eyes at me like I was a fool and shook her head. Then she pressed the palm of her hand against her chest. "But I'm still keeping an eye on him."

"Yeah, me too." I pumped a little sanitizer on my hands.

"Good. 'Cause I really want to know what's going on. And I have no problem flying solo if I have to."

I smelled my hands. "No, no. I wanna spy." Honestly, it wasn't so much about spying on Robachico. I liked hanging out with Vivi. She could be pretty mean sometimes, but I knew that would change if we became friends, like, real friends.

On Zoom, Mr. Z was talking about different earth formations, about earthquakes and volcanos. Vivi glanced at the screen for a moment, then she wrote something in a notebook and pushed it toward me.

Her handwriting was pretty, letters like little balloons: *Spy after school. Do NOT let Alita stop us.*

But the moment we closed the laptop after school, Alita called us over. "No, no. Por favor," she said. "It's going to rain."

"What?" Vivi went to the window and looked. "No it's not."

"Yes it is," Alita said, and patted the place on the couch next to her. "Come here and sit. Both of you."

"Alita, there's not even a cloud in the sky," Vivi said, and gave me this helpless look.

"Trust me, Viviana. Ándale. Come sit."

I sat on one side of Alita. Vivi plopped herself down on the other, crossed her arms, and pouted. She obviously wanted Alita—and the world—to know she was not happy about being there.

"Miren." Alita showed us a photograph of a big square stone statue. "This is Tlaloc, the god of rain. And he says it's going to rain today."

"So you talked to him?" Vivi said.

Alita ignored her. I pointed to the woman in front of the statue. "Who's that?"

"That young lady right there is me."

"You're dressed like Vivi," I said.

Vivi leaned forward and frowned at me.

"She's vintage," I said. In the picture, Alita wore a skirt and a pink handkerchief on her head and big dark glasses. She looked cool.

"Whatever." Vivi stood. "Let's go, Lalo."

"Por favor, Viviana." Alita tapped the photo a couple of times with her index finger. "I don't want you getting soaked."

"But, Alita . . ." Vivi sat again and crossed her arms. "It's not gonna rain."

"Óiganme bien," Alita said. "Tlaloc is the god of rain and fertility. The weatherman can tell you when it is going to rain. But Tlaloc is the one who makes it rain."

"Yeah, right," Vivi said. "Thanks for the lesson in superstition."

"Es verdad—it's true."

"He's a weird-looking god," I said. The statue was like this big square, didn't even look like a person.

"It's a very old statue," Alita explained, "carved by hand with primitive tools. It weighs almost two hundred tons. That is a very big stone."

"Yeah, that's a lot," Vivi said, and nodded toward the door.

"The Mexica people sacrificed children to Tlaloc so he would make it rain."

"Like, killed them for real?" I said.

Alita nodded and removed her little reading glasses from her nose. "They needed rain so the corn would grow."

"Oh, I get it," Vivi said sarcastically. "So, the magic won't work unless you sacrifice a few innocent children to a giant rock. Nice. Real nice."

"Those were ancient times," Alita said. "The Mexica were polytheistic people. They believed in different gods. Many of their rituals involved human sacrifices to keep the gods happy."

"That's so cool," I said.

Vivi glanced at me. "You think?"

I shrugged. "I wish we would learn this stuff at school instead of things like the Louisiana Purchase and the Bill of Rights and the War of 1812 and stuff."

"Listen to me, when they moved the statue of Tlaloc to Mexico City," Alita explained, "it rained nonstop for four days. It was the worst rainstorm in the city's history. And that was during the dry season, eh?"

"They must have sacrificed a ton of kids," Vivi said.

"Ay, Viviana. You always make fun of things. You should open your heart. This is your past. It belongs to you."

"I'm not sure that's a good thing," Vivi said. "I'd hate to be sacrificed in exchange for a few raindrops."

Alita shook her head. "If you don't believe in the power of your ancestors, you are only living half a life, niña."

"Do you believe in robachicos?" I said.

"Sí, claro," Alita said. "There were girls in my pueblo who were taken by el robachicos. But that has nothing to do with magic—"

"I told you," Vivi said.

"Los robachicos are as real as you and me," Alita explained. "Son gente mala. They steal children and sell them as servants or put them to work in the street selling Chiclets. That is a cruel and dirty business."

"But you always say Mexico is a wonderful place," I said.

"It is, mijo. But unfortunately no place is perfect. Not even Mexico."

"You think there could there be robachicos here?" I said, and glanced at Vivi.

"Claro. There are robachicos everywhere," Alita said. "That's why you children need to be careful and do what your parents tell you."

"There. Robachico's existence is officially confirmed." Vivi stood and motioned for me to follow.

"No, no, mija." Alita stopped her. "It's going to rain."

"Alita—"

"And you need to clean up that mess in your room."

"That's Lupe's mess," Vivi cried.

"No me importa," Alita said. "It's your room, too. Tell Lupe to help you."

Vivi gave me this angry look as if it was all my fault. Then she stomped away and into her room.

I walked out of Vivi's apartment and glanced at the parking lot. The motor home sat alone in the same place. The sky was clear except for a few clouds far away on the horizon.

That night, it rained.

12.

A couple of days later, our language arts teacher, Mrs. Panachek, gave us an assignment to keep a journal. She said we were living a very important moment in history, that the Covid pandemic and the lockdown would be something our grandchildren would learn about in school. "Just as my great-grandparents suffered during the flu pandemic of 1918, and my grandparents struggled through the Depression of the 1930s, and my parents lived through the Vietnam War and the civil rights movement of the 1960s, these are unprecedented times. It's up to us to keep an honest record of what our lives are like during the lockdown." She held a notebook up to the camera on her computer. "Write down what you do each and every day. Even the smallest details are important. For example, yesterday when I went to the grocery store, they were all out of toilet paper. That was completely unexpected."

"I really don't want to imagine Mrs. Panachek sitting in the toilet," Vivi whispered.

"Please," Mrs. Panachek went on. "While it is absolutely

vital that we keep a record of what is happening in our lives during this difficult time, it is also important that we express our feelings. This lockdown is not easy for any of us. Whether you're lonely or afraid or sad, writing down how we feel can help us understand what's going on in our heads and in our hearts and help us feel better."

I glanced at Vivi and back at the computer. The moment Mrs. Panachek turned away from the camera, I said to Vivi, "But nothing happens to us?"

She nodded and adjusted her mask. "I know. Except you smell your hands every time you use sanitizer."

At that exact moment, there was a knock on the door.

Alita set her embroidery aside and went out, leaving the door open a sliver. Before Covid, she would have invited the person inside. My mom, too. But not anymore. Alita stood outside on the walkway for a while. Vivi looked at me weird. Mrs. Panachek had moved on from the journal assignment and shared her screen, showing us a photograph of huge fancy-looking room that was like a palace or a museum. She wanted us to write a description of it.

Alita came back inside. She closed the door real gently and walked slowly to the kitchen. Her eyes had this faraway gaze, like when she stared at the wall and daydreamed about the past. She poured herself a glass of water but didn't drink it. She just stood there for a long time, staring at the Frida Kahlo magnet on the fridge.

Vivi looked at the image on the computer, then leaned forward and wrote, glanced at the screen and kept writing her description of the room with its tall columns and red couches and big paintings on the walls.

In the kitchen, Alita stood in the same place, just staring at the fridge. She brought her hand up and touched the side of her eye. Claudio was leaning over a textbook on the counter.

I went to the kitchen and touched Alita's arm. "Are you okay?"

She blinked a couple of times and gave me this empty stare. For a moment, it was as if she didn't even recognize me. She touched her eye again. That's when I saw it was a tear she was wiping before it ran down her cheek. She adjusted the top of her mask to make sure it covered her nose, took my hand, and led me back to the living room.

"Niños . . ." She cleared her throat. "Listen . . . por favor." She paused for a moment and let go of my hand. Then she spoke loud enough so Vivi and Claudio could hear. "There is some news . . . I need to share . . ." Her voice faltered. She cleared her throat again and said, "Don Frank—Don Frank is very sick with Covid. They took him to the clinic late last night. Irma said—she said—" She bowed her head and whispered, "It does not look good."

Alita's tone, her sadness, was like water. It soaked me from head to toe. But even then, it took a moment for the meaning of her words to sink in. Don Frank. Covid. Clinic.

Alita sat, her tiny body sinking deep into the big couch that seemed to swallow her whole as she crossed herself. Don Frank was her good friend. They were from the same town outside Mexico City. They knew the same people. Alita used to say, "That Don Frank knows more about what is going on back home than I ever will."

I opened my notebook and did what Mrs. Panachek told us to do. I wrote, *Don Frank got Covid. They took him away.*

Don Frank wasn't the first person in the building to get sick with Covid. Over a month ago—before the lockdown, when we didn't even know what Covid was, when they called it Corona and everyone made jokes because it was only happening in China—Ma had to call an ambulance for Mrs. Castro, who lived alone on our floor in the apartment next to the stairs. They thought it was just a bad cold or something. The paramedics took her away. Turned out it was Covid. We haven't seen her since.

I wanted to tell Alita everything would be fine. But it would be a lie. I didn't know if anything was ever going to be okay—not for Mrs. Castro or Don Frank or any of us. I didn't know anything about Covid—no one did. They just said to wear your mask, wash your hands, and stay six feet away. If you got it, you got sick. If you got it bad, you died.

There was nothing anyone could do. We couldn't help Don Frank just like we couldn't help Mrs. Castro. And seeing Alita so sad made me feel even worse. It was as if Covid was an invisible monster, a robachicos who took away anyone he wanted—stole people young and old and never gave them back.

Vivi stared at her notebook and turned the pages, one after another without paying attention, just kept flipping them like a machine, her eyes blank, her hand moving faster and faster.

"Vivi." I tapped her arm with my elbow.

She stopped and gave me this blank stare. "Don't you get it?" she said. "My mom . . . She works at the hospital. She's around people with Covid. And your mom, too. They—" She choked on her words. "They could get it, too." Then she dropped her head and cried.

I thought of what Alita had said about the black moth. But I hadn't seen a moth. Maybe Don Frank would be okay. Or maybe someone else saw a moth. And even if they did, then what? Alita said the moth was only a messenger.

My throat felt as if I were choking on a handful of sand. I tried to force it down, but it wouldn't go away. The sounds in the apartment disappeared, and for a moment I was alone. I could see myself as if I wasn't me. I was sitting next to Vivi staring at the computer like an idiot, but I wasn't really there. I was seeing myself from the outside. That person sitting at the dining room table was just my body. I was floating. My back pressed against the ceiling on the far side of the room near the front window. Everything that was happening was happening outside of me—Alita looking tiny in the middle of the giant couch; Claudio hunched over the counter, black hood over his big head, earbuds in; Vivi sitting with her head bowed, weeping quietly for Don Frank and her mom.

I got scared. What if I had Covid? Maybe I'd died and was floating up to heaven, except the ceiling got in the way. I thought of Ma, that I would never see her again. I breathed, sucked in air, swallowed it as if I'd just come up after being underwater for a long time.

And then, I was back in my chair.

I ran to the bathroom and locked the door and sat on the toilet, dropped my head in my hands and cried.

I don't know if it was for Don Frank or Alita or Ma or Covid or what. Everything that had been building and building and building finally came out of me in tears and sobs and a strange weeping sound I didn't recognize.

I hated Covid. I hated what it was doing to us. But I liked being on lockdown. I liked being here with Vivi and Alita. I guess I was angry at myself because the truth was that I didn't want it to end even if it wasn't fair to everyone else.

"Lalo?" Claudio knocked on the door. "You okay, bro?"

"Hold on." I blew my nose and washed my face. I didn't want Claudio to know I'd been crying. I didn't want him to make fun of me.

When I opened the door, he stood there with his hood over his head, his black mask over his mouth and nose. All I could see of him were his dark sad eyes, staring at me like he was going to say something stupid and mean, but he didn't. Instead, he put his arms around me and held me like I was falling, his body folding into mine.

He told me everything was going to be okay, even though we both knew it wasn't. And for the first time since I don't know when, I was glad Claudio was my brother even if he stank like stale Doritos.

13.

That afternoon, Ma still hadn't come home. I opened my notebook and studied the plan for turning the PS3 into a memory machine. I flipped through the pages and saw the notes I took in Mrs. Panachek's language arts class about keeping a journal—and what I wrote: *Don Frank got Covid. They took him away.* I thought of poor Don Frank and how happy he was at the end of the day when he handed us paletas from his little cart. You'd think he was the one getting a treat.

My notes said to put down my feelings, that expressing myself would help me feel better, but nothing came to me. It was as if I didn't feel anything. I just had this weird blank sense like a memory that wasn't there. I really wanted to write something important that said how I felt about my life right now, but I couldn't put it into words. There was so much going on and it was all jumbled up inside so that I couldn't figure it out—not in a way I could say. So all I wrote was *nothing*.

I stared at the word for a long time—*nothing*. Something about it wasn't right. It sounded mean—as if I didn't care or wasn't feeling anything. But it wasn't that. It was just that I was feeling everything at once. I scratched it out and wrote a new word, *numb*.

I went to the couch and watched the motor home for a while, but there was nothing going on. It was boring. There was nothing to do.

I went up to the roof and sat there for a long time just listening to the silence. The annoying buzz of traffic rushing on the highway behind the building was gone.

But as nice as the silence was, I kind of missed the regular sounds of life, of people laughing and arguing about whatever. It was almost creepy how everything seemed dead. Except nature. Weeds grew in the cracks in the pavement below, and the breeze and humidity had this clean smell of earth and grass. I took my mask off and breathed it in. It was so different from before. I could even smell the salt of the ocean. I wanted to remember it forever, but I knew I probably wouldn't.

"What are you doing?"

Lupe. She was dressed like a vampire—black jeans, black shirt, black boots, long black hair—even her fingernails were painted black.

"Nothing."

She took her mask off.

"Don't get too close," I said.

"I know." She sat cross-legged about ten feet away from me. We stared at each other.

I don't know why, but Lupe scared me. Maybe because Claudio always said she was psycho and she always kept to herself.

She was older and had this look about her as if she knew something no one else did.

"I saw you from the parking lot," she said. The breeze blew her hair across her face. She shook her head to get it out of her eyes and curled a strand behind her ear. "It's nice up here, no?"

I nodded. "It's quiet."

"It sucks about Don Frank."

The mention of his name brought back that weird feeling like I was separating from my body. I focused on my hands to make the feeling go away. Yesterday's notes were half washed out. But I had a new one about spying on Robachico written just above my wrist. I traced the lines the pen made on my brown skin, the loops of my handwriting, then on the folds of my mask, pulled on one of the straps.

Lupe must have sensed I was uncomfortable because she changed the subject. "So, you come up here a lot?"

"Sometimes."

"It's a long way down."

"Four stories."

"You'd die if you jumped," she said.

I thought about that all the time, how you'd die if you fell headfirst and broke your neck or cracked your skull. If you jumped feetfirst you might survive. Maybe. Not that I would do it.

"I'm not gonna jump," I said.

"I didn't say you were."

"I wonder if it would hurt," I said. "Like if you fell and died, would it hurt first?"

She cracked a tiny smile that disappeared as quickly as it had come. "I think the same thing."

"It would be like a second or two of pain and then you're dead, no?"

"I guess."

The wind blew and she turned her head to face it and curled her hair behind her ears. "I get so tired of sitting inside," she said. "Makes me feel like a prisoner. Stupid lockdown, no?"

The back of her hand was covered with line drawings of vines and flowers.

"You got a tattoo?" I said.

She glanced at her hand, fiddled with her bracelet that looked like a bicycle chain but in shiny chrome or maybe silver, kept turning it around her wrist. She wore a lot of jewelry, a crucifix around her neck, rings on her fingers—all silver.

"Maybe one day," she said, and held her hand up, turned it in front of me. "These are just doodles. I do them with a pen."

"Pretty cool."

"Makes the time go by during class."

I glanced at my hand, the dark skin, washed-out words. "I write notes to myself," I said, and showed her my hand.

"Is that because of your problem?" she said.

"I don't have a problem."

"My amá says you need special help with your schoolwork and stuff. That's why my grandmother babies you all the time."

"She doesn't baby me," I cried. "She's teaching me Spanish and about Mexico."

She shook her head and turned to face the breeze so that it blew her hair away from her face. "Whatever."

I bowed my head. My hands had turned into fists. It was automatic, like a reflex. Anytime something about my memory came up, I tensed up like a knot. I opened my hand and faked a yawn to loosen my jaw.

Lupe closed her eyes. I couldn't take my eyes away from her. She looked so nice, pretty with her face tilted back a little, lips dark but slightly upturned in a smile. I didn't understand how she could be such a jerk. But for some strange reason, despite everything she said, I wasn't angry at her. I didn't even feel that other thing, the one like a giant hand pressing me down and squeezing me so hard it made it difficult to breathe.

"Why're you so mean?" I said.

Her eyes popped open. "I'm not mean." She smiled and rocked back and forward a couple of times. "I'm a chingona."

"What's that?"

"You'll find out," she said, and stared at me as if she was waiting for me to say something else, but I said nothing because I didn't know what to say to that. So she closed her eyes again, a peaceful expression on her face, like she was satisfied with herself.

A part of me was glad she was here, talking to me. But it felt weird. Like, I wanted to leave but I also wanted to stay. Made me wish I had my notebook so I could take notes, try to put something cool in my journal. But I didn't even have a pen to write on my hand and save the memory for later.

"So, if you're Mexican, how come you're black?" she said, her eyes still closed, her hair blowing in the breeze.

"I'm not black. I'm dark brown. And my dad was Haitian."

I turned toward the motor home and the parking lot and the street—deserted. I hated that, how people didn't believe I was Mexican. They always thought I was Cuban or Dominican because my skin was so dark. But the Haitians at school didn't believe I was Haitian because I didn't speak Creole.

"So, what about your problem then?" she said, changing the subject again. "Vivi said you were in special classes."

"They're not special classes, they're accommodations."

"What's that then?"

"They just give me more time to work on tests and stuff."

"Because of your problem."

"I told you, it's not a problem. I just don't remember stuff."

She opened her eyes. "It's gotta suck, no?"

"What do you care?"

"I don't," she said. "I'm just curious. I'd hate it if I couldn't remember stuff." She looked down at her bracelet again, turned it around and around, the silver shining against her black fingernails. "You remember your dad?"

I didn't. That was the worst part of not remembering. But I didn't want to tell her because I didn't want her to feel sorry for me. I hated it when people felt sorry for me.

"My dad's in Mexico," she said before I could answer her question.

"Vivi told me. She said he's stuck there because of Covid."

"He's not coming back."

"Ever?"

She shrugged.

"Why?"

She shrugged again, focused on her bracelet. "If I tell you something, you promise not to tell?"

"I'll probably forget it anyway."

She laughed and raised her eyes, looked at me for the first time in a while. "I have a boyfriend."

"That's cool." I smiled, but when I looked down, I noticed my hands were clenched. "Why's that a secret?"

"I didn't say it was. I just don't want you to tell anyone."

"Doesn't that make it a secret?"

"Whatever."

I kept stealing glances at her but didn't want her to catch me, so I just kept moving my eyes back and forth from the parking lot to her eyes. "So, how come you don't speak Spanish?"

"Who said I didn't?"

"No one," I said. "But Vivi's always flipping from English to Spanish."

"Don't let Vivi fool you. She was just a baby when we came here. Alita taught her what little Spanish she knows."

"But she knows a lot."

"She just talks that pocho crap. I speak real Spanish. I just don't mix it with English like she does, okay?" She stood, put her mask back on, and walked away.

When she got to the secret stairs, she stopped. "Oye. And just because we talked doesn't mean we're friends."

I pushed myself away from the edge of the roof and lay on

my back, stared at the sky and tried to think of my father. But it was all a blank. I couldn't remember his voice, how he laughed, what he smelled like. All I had were images—the same ones from the photos in the house—my father in soft faded colors, Papi in little paper rectangles.

14.

In the days after they took Don Frank away, no one talked much. Vivi didn't say anything about spying on Robachico. And Alita—she didn't mention Don Frank or Covid. There were no more stories, no more Mexican magic. She didn't even stare into space or talk to José or anything. It was as if she no longer suffered from nostalgia. She just sat on the couch and embroidered her masks in silence.

But all that changed when Sunday showed up with a bucket of giant mangoes. His real name's Domingo—Spanish for "Sunday." But Vivi called him Sunday. She did that, changed people's names from Spanish to English. Like Flor de María, who lived in the apartment next door to her. Vivi called her Flower of Mary.

Classes had almost wrapped up when Alita met Sunday at the door. They stood outside on the walkway, a few feet apart, masks over their faces. I was afraid Sunday had come to tell us that someone else was in the hospital with Covid. Or that Don Frank had died. But instead, he set a bucket of mangoes on the ground between him and Alita. "They're from my sister's trees," he said. "I figured the children might enjoy them."

Alita's eyes lit up for the first time since Don Frank was taken away. "Pero son muchos, Domingo. Are you sure?"

"Sí, por favor. We have a stand on the side of the road down in Naples, but things are very quiet."

"El lockdown."

"Ey. They're just about ripe. It would be a shame if they went to waste."

"Bueno, in that case," Alita said, "I'm happy to take them. I'm sure we'll enjoy them—and not just the children, eso sí."

Sunday nodded and took his hat off. "Y, por favor, tell your daughter we appreciate all the work she's doing at the hospital. It must be very difficult for her . . . and for you and the girls. She and Margarita are real heroes. Que Dios las bendiga."

Alita had Claudio carry the bucket to the kitchen, and she got to work right away. She was an expert—made you think she'd owned a fruit stand back in Mexico or something. She stabbed a fork into the bottom of each mango for a handle and peeled them like a banana with a knife—three quick swipes and she was done. Then she sliced the flesh halfway all around them so the mangos looked like flowers, just like the ones they sold at the Cinco de Mayo fair in Immokalee. She even squeezed lime all over them and sprinkled them with Tajín.

She marched out of the kitchen with a mango in each hand like two giant yellow lollipops. She gave one each to Vivi and me and pointed at the door. "Afuera, por favor—outside. I don't want a sticky mess in here. Vayan, pues."

We went up to the roof and sat facing the parking lot. We chomped on the mangoes like they were our last meal. They were so good, sweet and tart with the lime and spice from the Tajín, just like Mexican candy. We ate and laughed so hard with our mouths full, sticky mango juice dripping down our chins, so that for a moment if felt as if we were real friends and there was no pandemic, no lockdown. No Covid. No Robachico.

"Idea!" Vivi announced, her face and hands wet and sticky with mango juice. "Let's plant the bones and grow our own trees."

"They're pits."

"What?"

"They're not bones," I said. "They're pits."

"Dude. El hueso del mango. That's how you say it."

"Not in English."

"I know," she said, and glanced at where her shirt was stained with mango juice. "But it's the same thing."

"No, it's not."

"Whatever."

When we finished, we pulled the pits off the forks and set them on the ground to dry. I wiped my lips with my sleeve and put my mask back on.

Vivi sucked her fingers one at a time. "So, how's your time machine coming?"

"It's not a time machine. It's a memory machine."

"Well, it should be," she said, and pulled a few loose hairs away from her face with her pinky. "I mean, how can you remember things without going to the past. Besides, wouldn't that be cool?"

"You remember all the time," I said. "And you don't go back in time."

"Yeah, but that's different."

"Memory and time are two different things," I said.

"I guess."

"Anyway, I don't even know if the hard drive is usable," I said. "But if I can't store my memories, I might at least be able to project them."

"That would be cool."

"It's like this dream I had."

She frowned. "I thought you couldn't remember stuff?"

"I remember some things. Like, I only remember parts of the dream. I was in Mexico and—"

"Dude, you've never been."

"I know. It's probably because of Alita's stories. Anyway, there was a cat. I was in a street and there was this black-and-white cat standing in the middle of a street, staring at me. Someone was crying."

"Why?"

"I don't know," I said. "That's why I want the memory machine."

"How do you know it was in Mexico?"

"I don't. It just felt like it, like I was in one of Alita's stories or something."

"Honestly," she said, "I can never remember my dreams."

I smiled. "I guess we have something in common."

She ignored my comment and glanced at the mango pits. "So, we gonna plant them, o qué?"

"Sure."

"We'll have our own trees," she said.

"And we can sell them on the street like Sunday. We'll be rich."

"Sunday's not rich."

She had a point. I grabbed my fork and glanced at the parking lot, nodded at the motor home. "You think Sunday gave Robachico some mangoes?"

"Maybe he doesn't like them."

"Everyone likes mangoes."

"Some people don't," she said, and got real serious. "Besides, Robachico only eats children."

"Right." I laughed. "And he probably puts a little lime and sprinkles Tajín before eating them."

"Oh my God!" Vivi cried. "I have the best idea ever. Let's put a mango in front of Robachico's door, knock on the door, and run."

"Why?"

"So he'll come out. We'll finally get to see him."

15.

We went back to Vivi's apartment and washed off all the sticky juice from our hands and faces. Vivi ran into her room to change, came out wearing camo pants and a tie-dyed polo shirt that was too big for her but made her look cool. She grabbed a big green-and-reddish mango from the bucket, and we sat at the dining room table, where we did our schoolwork.

"We should write a note," she said.

"Why?"

"So he knows it's from us."

"So, we're knocking on his door and running away," I said, "but we're letting him know it was us?"

"Good point. He might get mad."

"You think?"

Alita checked us out over her little reading glasses. She went back to her embroidering but kept stealing glances at us every now and then.

Vivi ripped a page from her notebook and tapped the front of her mask with a pencil. "What should we say?"

"I don't know."

"How about, Dear Mr.— No, wait. We can't just say Mr. Robachico."

We laughed.

"Say neighbor. Dear neighbor . . ."

She leaned over the page and wrote slowly, whispering each word as she put it down on paper. "Dear neighbor, please accept this mango as a gift. We hope you like it."

She sat up and studied the note, then the mango. "How do we attach it?"

"Here." I folded the note and placed it on top of the mango. "We need tape."

Vivi ran to the kitchen and searched the cabinets.

Alita put down her embroidery and sighed. "¿Qué buscas, niña?"

"Tape."

"We don't have any."

"What about rubber bands?"

"I don't know what that is." Alita adjusted her reading glasses and started on her embroidery again.

Vivi stomped back to the table and sat. "How do you say 'rubber bands' in Spanish?"

"I know," I said. "Let's write the note on the mango."

"Lalo." She reached across the table and pressed my cheeks with her hands. "You're a genius!"

She copied what was on the note onto the mango with a black Sharpie. "Should we sign it?"

"You sign it if you want," I said, "but leave my name out of it."

She tapped her mask with the end of the Sharpie a couple of times. Then she leaned over and drew a happy face. She turned the mango around so I could see it right side up. "At least this way he'll know were friendly."

She grabbed the mango and we started for the door, but Alita stopped us. "Viviana . . ."

"We're just going to the parking lot real quick."

"No, mi vida. Ya es tarde," Alita said. "You have homework."

"I'll do it later."

"You have to do it now because you also have to shower. Tu mamá is coming home tonight and we are having dinner together."

"Ay, Alita, por favor. Five minutes . . ."

Alita glanced at her wristwatch. "No, mi amor. You can play tomorrow."

Vivi huffed and handed me the mango. "You do it."

"It's cool." I offered it back to her. "We can do it tomorrow."

"Come on, Lalo—"

"It was your idea."

"Dude, just set it on the ground in front of the door, knock, and run home," she said. "It's no big deal."

"Yeah, easy for you to say."

"Whatever." She took the mango from me and moved her hands around it as if she was feeling its weight. "I knew you'd chicken out."

"Hey!"

"You always do."

"No, I don't. I just think we should do it together."

"He probably won't even come out."

"But what if he does?" I said.

"He won't."

"But if he does—"

"Just run. Knock on the door and run. He won't even see you." She handed me the mango. "It'll be fine. Trust me."

When I walked out of Vivi's apartment, I stood on the walkway and looked over the railing at the parking lot. It was getting dark. The motor home sat like always, small and ugly and creepy. But for some reason, it seemed scarier, like something from a horror movie.

I went downstairs. Socrates was gathering his tools. He closed the hood of the car he was working on with a loud clap—made me jump. The rest of the parking lot was deserted. No witnesses. No one to help me.

I walked slowly, held the mango in front of me with both hands like it was a giant egg. With each step the motor home seemed to get bigger. I could hear Claudio's voice in the back of my head: *Crimes against humanity. Robachico. Monster . . . Monster!*

As I got closer, I got a whiff of something gross like trash or rotting fruit. I looked down at the mango, Vivi's handwriting, the thick lines of the Sharpie, the perfect smiley face like an emoji. I kept telling myself there was nothing to be afraid of. I didn't believe in Robachico. Besides, this mango was a gift—a nice thing. There was no reason for him to get angry. Still, my heart pounded hard and fast against my chest. And Claudio's words wouldn't stop: *Monster. Monster. Monster!*

I stopped a couple of feet from the motor home. A faded yellow curtain covered the window. There was something red on the door handle—maybe blood. I set the mango on the ground by the step, raised my hand, and knocked real fast—*tap-tap-tap*—and ran away as fast as I could.

16.

The next morning when Ma got home from work, she shook me awake. "Good morning, sunshine."

I sat up on the couch. "What day is it?"

"Saturday," she said, and ruffled my hair. "Why did you sleep out here?"

She was in her uniform, purple pants and a colorful shirt with bunnies and flowers, her face marked with the red outline around her cheeks and nose. N95 masks left deep marks on her face. But worse, they had to keep reusing them because Ma said they didn't have a good supply. Sometimes she even had to wear two regular surgical masks one over the other. They didn't leave big marks like the N95s, but Ma said they hurt the back of her ears.

"I don't know." I went to her bedroom and sat on her bed and waited for her to come out of the bathroom.

When she came in, she lay on the bed faceup. She smelled of sweat and perfume and medicine. Her eyes were red and droopy and sad.

"Cream?"

"No, thank you, mi amor."

"Ma . . . can you tell me about Papi?"

"Can we do this later?" She put on her eye mask to help her sleep and took my hand. "I'm too tired. I need to sleep."

In our room, Claudio was sprawled on his bed sleeping, hadn't even taken his clothes off—hoodie and all. I studied the poster board with the parts for my memory machine. I thought of what Vivi had said about it being a time machine. She said to remember was to go back in time. But that was impossible. To go back in time, you'd have to be physically in the past. The memory machine was only going to help me remember things that already happened. Besides, it couldn't go to the future. But if for some reason the memory machine turned out like a time machine and took me to the past, maybe I could help Don Frank. I wondered where he got Covid. After they took Mrs. Castro away, we were all super careful, even Don Frank, although he wasn't wearing a mask the last time I saw him.

I went to the kitchen and poured myself what was left of the Cap'n Crunch and ate. I was hoping I would remember everything from yesterday, or why I ended up on the couch. I glanced at my hand, but there was nothing written on it. Nothing came to me.

Maybe Alita knew of some special Mexican magic that might help Don Frank. We couldn't go to the hospital to visit him, but magic was magic. I didn't see why it wouldn't work remotely, like Zoom.

I grabbed the binoculars and stepped out of the apartment. Vivi was just coming down the walkway. She wore a plaid skirt, Converse high-tops and a *Rick and Morty* T-shirt. "Did he come out?"

"Who?" We leaned against the railing in front of my apartment and looked out at the parking lot.

"Who do you think?" She took the binoculars from me and checked the motor home. "Well, he took the mango."

"What mango?"

She put the binoculars down and frowned. "Dude, are you for real right now? Yesterday, Sunday brought us a bucket of mangoes. ¿No te acuerdas? We ate them on the roof."

"Yeah. We're going to plant the pits, right?"

"The bones," she said. "But we also wrote a note on a mango. You were supposed to put it in front of Robachico's door."

"For real?"

"Yeah, and knock on his door."

"Why me?"

"Lalo!"

"Did I do it?"

"No sé. The mango's not there. You think—" She narrowed her eyes. "Maybe you saw him but forgot?"

I turned and squinted at the motor home. I didn't want to think I'd seen Robachico and forgotten. But I'd forgotten more important things. All I could remember from yesterday was eating mangoes on the roof—then I woke up on the couch.

"Wouldn't it be funny," Vivi said, "if you actually met him and had a conversation and everything and now you can't remember?"

"How's that even funny?" I hated that. I hated forgetting. It was as if parts of my life never happened.

17.

We went up to Vivi's apartment. Alita was sitting at her sewing machine by the window.

"Do we have any empty cans?" Vivi asked.

Alita put on her mask and leaned back on her chair. "What do I know about cans, mija?"

"Like for beans or pozole." Vivi held her hands up to show her the size of the cans she wanted. "You know, the big ones."

"Look in the trash or the recycle bin." Alita followed her to the kitchen. "What are you up to that you need empty cans?"

"We're going to plant our mango bones."

I dabbed some disinfectant on my hands and sat on the couch. Alita pulled a couple of cans from under the sink and handed them to Vivi.

"Alita," I said before she sat at her sewing machine. "Can I ask you a quick question?"

She placed her hands on her waist. "Sí, claro."

"Is there any Mexican magic that can cure people?"

"Lalo," Vivi called from the kitchen, where she was rinsing out the cans. "Don't start. We're leaving in two minutes."

Alita sat beside me and petted my knee. "Claro que sí. La curandera. She uses herbs and diets and plenty of ancient magic. She can cure almost anything."

"Is that kind of like a witch doctor?"

"Not at all." She laughed. "She's a healer. She knows everything about how to use plants and teas made from obscure herbs to cure illnesses like indigestion, bone pains, that sort of thing. But she can also treat uncommon illnesses like broken hearts, laziness, and bad moods."

"What about Covid?"

Alita shook her head. "Not as far as I know. Just look at us locked up in here wearing masks like doctors and nurses."

"What about the magic?" I didn't want to bring up Don Frank because I knew it would hurt her to remember.

"I suppose it's possible," she said. "Cuando era niña, before we moved to the city, we used to dig for Aztec artifacts in my uncle's milpa. We usually found bits of pottery or obsidian arrowheads in his cornfield. But one day my friend Leticia found a small black colibrí—a hummingbird carved of obsidian rock. In Aztec mythology these little birds had healing powers because of their relationship to the sun and the god Huitzilopochtli. We didn't think much of it. But one day Leticia's cousin Fernanda, who always suffered from reverse insomnia, came down with a case of sadness even the doctors didn't know how to treat."

"An uncommon illness."

"Exactly," she said. "The doctors were helpless. And the curandera tried everything, but nothing worked. They feared that if she kept sleeping like that, she might never recover."

"So"—Vivi came out of the kitchen, a can in each hand—"Leticia held the bird in her hands, said the magic words, and Fernanda woke up."

Alita shook her head. "It wasn't so simple. Leticia and I kept an eye on Fernanda day and night. Every time she tried to turn over in her sleep, we straightened her out so she would lie faceup like the curandera told us we should do. For no particular reason, Leticia placed the little bird on Fernanda's hand. The moment she did that, Fernanda's body levitated."

"She flew?

"No, no. She just floated about this high above the bed." Alita held her hand up flat about a foot above the couch. "Nos dio un susto. She stayed like that for a few minutes, maybe half an hour. We had never seen anything like it. I wanted to call the priest, but Leticia said it would be better to take a picture. Unfortunately, there was no film in her sister's camera. Then Fernanda came down slowly back to the bed and woke up."

"Was she cured?" Vivi asked.

Alita nodded. "Fully recovered."

"The hummingbird," I said. "Mexican magic. I knew it."

"Cool," Vivi said, and walked to the door. "Lalo, come on. We have work to do."

When we walked out of the apartment, Vivi handed me one of the cans. "You really believe that nonsense?"

"Sure. Why not?"

"I think she's losing it in here," she said, and touched her temple with her index finger.

On our way up to the secret stairs, we found Misty Blue standing outside her apartment, smoking a cigarette. Misty had been living in the building since forever. She was skinny like a skeleton, had long gray hair, and always wore these long flowing dresses. Everyone said she owned like ten cats, but I'd never seen one. When I was little, I was afraid of her because I thought she was a witch.

She was standing on the walkway, leaning on the rail, staring at the parking lot. When she saw us come up, she blew a cloud of smoke and smiled. "What's going on, kids?"

"We're planting mango trees," I said.

"It's the strangest thing." Misty pointed to the parking lot with her cigarette. "There's a motor home over there."

"It's been there for days," Vivi said.

"I hadn't noticed it before."

"It's a ghost motor home," I said.

Misty laughed and coughed. Then she pointed at me with her cigarette. "You might be right, son."

"Do you know who lives there?" Vivi asked.

"No. But last night there was a mango right there in front of the darn thing. And now it's gone."

"Wha-what—" Vivi stuttered. "What happened to it?"

"I suppose someone ate it." Misty scratched the side of her

head with her thumb, then pointed her cigarette at us. "Listen, I've been thinking we should make a banner."

"For the motor home?" I said.

"No, silly, for your moms." Misty spread her arms like Jesus Christ. "We can make a huge colorful banner with a slogan like, HEROES LIVE HERE. Maybe those kids that are always spray-painting the building can give us a hand."

"Yeah, sounds cool." Vivi stepped forward to pass.

"Yeah, and maybe"—Misty stopped her—"maybe we could have your sister help out. I'm sure Lupe would enjoy it. And it might help her, you know, like art therapy. Give her a chance to—"

"We gotta go—"

"Or the banner can say WE LOVE OUR HEROES," Misty went on. "That's better. We can paint flowers on it, make it real color-ful, like a genuine piece of art. Oh, it'll be so beautiful. Your moms will love it."

"Sounds good," I said.

"We gotta get through." Vivi made her way past Misty. I followed.

"We're going to need a big canvas," Misty said. "We can hang it across the front of the building. Everyone'll see it. They'll know who we are, that we have heroes . . ." And she went on like that talking to herself.

18.

The roof was bright and hot, felt like summer. At the far end, three guys in hoodies and big bright tennis shoes stood in a circle, probably smoking or drinking—doing something they weren't supposed to, for sure.

I froze. "Claudio."

"So?" Vivi nudged me with her elbow and marched to where we left our mango pits.

I followed but kept my eyes on Claudio. He was with Hugo and Jesse. Hugo was the worst. He was huge, taller than Claudio, all muscles and fat—probably psycho, too. And even worse, his dad was Nazario—the property manager and the man who collected rent. Hugo got away with everything.

I could hear them talking, something about the motor home. It sounded serious, as if they were making a plan. Hugo said they should take action, deal with it once and for all. Jesse said the guy was nuts, that he could kill everyone in the building.

"What the heck?" The mango pits were gone.

I shook my head because I knew Vivi, and I knew what she was going to do. But she did it anyway.

"Hey!" she called.

Claudio and them turned at the same time. They weren't wearing masks.

"You steal our mango bones?" Vivi yelled.

Claudio looked at Hugo. Jesse looked at Claudio. Hugo grinned at us—but not in a good way.

They started toward us.

I stepped back. Vivi set her can down and placed her hands on the sides of her waist, like Wonder Woman, raised her chin. "Entonces, did you, or what?"

Hugo walked right up to her, stood inches away. "What about it, chanchita?"

"Look who's talking," Vivi said. "Marrano asqueroso."

Claudio shoved me. "You ask Ma about Papi, fool?"

"No, I didn't."

"Why can't you leave her alone?"

"Where. Are. Our. Mango. Bones?" Vivi demanded.

"They're pits," Jesse corrected her. Hugo laughed, crossed his arms, kept grinning at Vivi.

"Every time you ask her about Papi, you're hurting her," Claudio went on. "It makes her cry. Can't you get that through your thick skull?" He smacked me on the side of the head.

"Don't touch me!"

"You forget what she tells you," he said. "But she doesn't. She cried all morning."

"I didn't say anything!"

"Ya, lárguense." Hugo waved us off. "Get off the roof."

"What about our mango bones?" Vivi said.

"We threw them away," Jesse said. "Now get off our roof."

"You don't even live in the building," I cried.

"But I do." Claudio pushed me.

"It's our roof now," Hugo said, his lip curled up like a snarling dog. "And you two jokers are not allowed up here. And your devil-worshipping sister, too. So, get off. Lárguense."

"Lupe doesn't worship a damn thing," Vivi said.

"I don't give a crap," Hugo said, and tapped his head with the palm of his hand. "Your crazy hermana needs a good spanking, thinks she's something special."

"Or send her to the nuthouse," Jesse said.

"Shut the hell up!" Vivi cried.

"Get off or I'll throw you off."

Vivi waved a finger in Hugo's face. "You don't own the building."

Hugo shoved Vivi. "My pop runs it." Then he poked my chest with his big fat finger. "And you, just 'cause you ain't got no father's no excuse for disrespecting your brother. He's older. He's in charge now, get it?"

"You don't know squat about my father!" I cried.

"Get off!" He pushed Vivi again, then pushed me. "You too, fool."

Claudio forced a laugh, his mouth twisted in a strange way, like half angry and half laughing.

"I'm gonna count to three." Hugo pushed me again. "One."

I shut my eyes. My body turned into a rock, my hands curled into fists.

"Two."

I charged Hugo and swung my arm as hard as I could. But he caught my fist like in a kung fu movie and twisted my arm, forced me to turn and kneel at his feet.

"Stop!" I yelled. He held my arm up against my back. Pain shot from my shoulder down my elbow. "You're breaking my arm!"

Claudio and Jesse stood there like idiots. I wanted to kill Hugo.

"Get off the roof," Hugo barked, "or I'll throw you over and give your mamá something to cry about for real. You get that?"

I was on my knees, my arm twisted, my hand just above the middle of my back, shoulder burning. And there was nothing I could do. Then I saw Vivi. Her eyes had this alien look I'd never seen before—fear and pity and something else I couldn't recognize—it was as if she didn't even know me. And everyone treating me like I didn't matter.

I don't know if it was the pain or what he said about my father or my mother or the humiliation or the feeling of help-lessness—I blanked out.

Vivi later told me I went totally loco. She said I started screaming in a voice that didn't sound like me. "Go ahead. Throw me!" I screamed it over and over like I was crazy. "Throw me! Throw me—Throw me—Throw me—Throw me!"

She said Hugo's face twisted and his eyes grew so wide she thought they were going to pop out of his ugly face. He glanced at my brother and then pushed me away from the edge of the roof. Then I sat up, panting. Vivi said I was foaming at the mouth, that I was getting ready to charge Hugo again, but she stopped me.

She grabbed me, held my arms from behind. "Don't." She pulled me back, led me to the secret stairs. "Come on, Lalo. Just forget it."

19.

The moment turned and turned in my head: Hugo and Jesse and Claudio laughing at me like a pack of hyaenas. The panic in Vivi's eyes. And Hugo talking trash about my mom, trying to school me like he was my dad. I wanted to go back and kill them, throw them over—do something. But I was just a skinny little kid, not even twelve years old, against three overfed, hormonal teenagers with no brains. I was helpless.

The whole way down the stairs Vivi stared ahead at nothing. I didn't know it then, but it wasn't because of what had just happened on the roof or because of the mango bones or because of Hugo. It was me.

"Take it easy." Her tone was short and squeaky. "It's cool, it's . . . okay."

"Don't—"

"Cálmate." She placed her hand on my back. "Forget about it."

"You don't get it!" I was always getting pushed around as if I didn't matter. And she was making it worse by acting like my mother, telling me to take it easy when it wasn't even my fault.

When we finally made it to the parking lot, she said, "Dude, you shouldn't have charged Hugo like that."

"*What!?*" I stepped away from her. "He started it."

"Yeah but—"

"Whose side are you on, anyway?"

Socrates poked his head out from under the hood of a car he was fixing. He was shirtless and covered in grease and sweat. He stared at us.

"You scared the crap out of me," Vivi said. "You went totally psycho—"

"Don't say that!" I cried.

"Oye, oye. ¿Qué pasa?" Socrates said.

"We're fine," Vivi barked at him. Then she pulled up her mask that had slipped below her nose. "Lalo, you need to chill."

"Don't tell me what to do!"

"Hey, hey, niños." Socrates gestured at us with a wrench. "Ya, no fighting, eh?"

"We're not!" Vivi said. But we were. Totally. She was all red in the face, and I was on the verge of tears.

"I expect this from your sister but not you, Viviana. Take it easy, okay?"

Vivi stepped closer to me and crossed her arms. "You're being a jerk."

"No," I cried. "You are. Hugo was gonna break my arm."

"No, he wasn't."

"How would you know?"

"I'm just trying to help," she said.

"Well, don't, okay?" I pushed her away and ran off. I wanted to disappear, fly way up in the sky like the voladores Alita talked about, go past the clouds where no one would bother me, or escape through some secret door to Mexico, to one of those magical places where the monarch butterflies made your wishes come true. Nobody got it. Not even Vivi.

I ran around to the side of the building where Irma was sitting on a chair outside the laundry room. Beto and Eric were pushing each other on a Big Wheel with no pedals.

I slowed down and wandered to the back of the building. Along the alley, a chain-link fence separated our building from the street that runs parallel to the highway above. A dresser without drawers and a broken table lamp sat in front of the two green dumpsters that were tagged with a bunch of graffiti.

I wanted to keep walking, go far away from here. There used to be a hole in the fence that made a shortcut to the field on the other side of the highway, but Nazario repaired it last Christmas. There was no way out the back. Besides, we were on lockdown. And I couldn't leave. I couldn't do that to Ma. She already put up with too much crap.

I sat on a cinder block and stared at our building, a stack of wooden pallets set against the wall, an old toilet, part of a pink laundry basket, and a few empty beer cans scattered on the ground. Originally, the wall had a pretty cool mural of a kid dressed like a little gangster, with pants that were too big for him, a baseball cap, and Nikes like the ones Claudio wore. Next to him was a young man in a business suit looking real proud. Above it, big balloon-like letters that seemed to shine spelled out the word DREAM.

But Claudio and those guys had ruined the lower part of the mural with graffiti—a bunch of lines and words that didn't make sense. Now it was just a mess of color, as if they were all screaming over each other, making it impossible to understand what they were saying.

A semitruck rumbled overhead on the highway. A homeless man crossed the street. He disappeared around the corner by the parking lot, then reappeared around the corner and came to the alley. He peeked in the dumpsters.

I got this weird feeling as if I'd been here before. If it hadn't just happened, I would have thought it was a memory, maybe one of those moments you remember with your heart, like Vivi said about nostalgia—you smell something that makes you feel a memory of someone or a place. You can't remember, but it rests on the tip of your tongue; you can feel it, but you can't figure it out no matter how hard you try.

The homeless man leaned into one of the dumpsters and pulled out a dirty blue backpack with one strap. He inspected it, moved the zippers back and forth. He tossed it over his shoulder and walked away the same way he came. Didn't even see me.

I crossed the alley to where the pallets were stacked against the wall and had set my foot up to climb on them when I saw a door. I'd never noticed it before, probably because it was covered in graffiti. It had a lock hanging on one side of the latch, but it had been torn off, screws and all.

I looked left, then right. There was no one around. I flicked the latch and pulled the door open.

20.

The room was like a cave. It was small and dark and stank of old paper and pee. I had never been scared of the dark—Ma said it was because there was nothing to fear in the dark—but I think it's because I didn't have any memories of bad things in the dark. This place was different. I wasn't supposed to be here. If Nazario found me, he might evict us—or worse—have me arrested for trespassing.

My eyes adjusted to the dark. There were a couple old stoves and a refrigerator without a door and a bunch of cardboard boxes all covered in dust. Don Frank's bike was parked next to an old AC window unit. At the opposite end of the room there was another door, probably to the laundry room.

I flicked a switch on the wall. It turned on a single bulb that hung on a wire in the middle of the room. I pulled the door closed behind me and walked farther into the room. I looked in the boxes. One had a bunch of books and magazines. Another box had clothes—a few T-shirts, jeans, boots. Vivi would love this stuff—vintage for sure.

I wished we hadn't argued, but I didn't do anything. It wasn't fair. She didn't have to treat me like a little kid, telling me to take it easy. I hated that. I wasn't some helpless loser. Maybe I had a temper, but so did everyone else. Besides, Hugo was a total jerk. He had no right to talk about my father like that. And he almost broke my arm for real.

At the far end of the room there was a typewriter on top of some dusty boxes next to a huge clothes dryer like the ones in the laundry room but twice as big. There was a bunch of other stuff scattered around—a black case, part of a bed frame, a stack of hubcaps, a big television with a curved glass screen, and a couple of small paintings and a big framed picture of the ocean. It was pretty cool—had these dramatic clouds as if a storm was brewing.

I sat on a microwave that was missing a door and dropped my head in my hands, shut my eyes. I wished I was older, stronger so I could fight back against Hugo and actually win. I was so tired of having this constant fear—a squiggly feeling that turned and turned in my stomach. I wished I could remember stuff that happened so people wouldn't talk over me like I didn't exist.

When I opened my eyes, it took me a moment to realize where I was. Behind a bunch of cardboard boxes, I noticed a big wooden cabinet almost as tall as me. The wood was carved real nice so it looked like it had two columns on the sides. The corners were curved and smooth, but it didn't have any drawers or doors or anything. The bottom half had two long rectangular shapes cut out and a pair of dusty brown cloths covering them like an old skirt. The top half had this triangular thing on the front, same shape as the piece you move on a Ouija board but a little bigger than my hand. I wiped the dust off. It was glass, slightly curved like a jewel, black background and a bunch of white writing on it that didn't make any sense—numbers in different sizes and random words like the names of countries GERMANY, FRANCE, HOLLAND, and U.S.A. plus POLICE and SHORT WAVE and VOICE and stuff. ZENITH was printed at an angle like a lightning bolt. My guess was that it was some type of old radio or something, but it didn't have AM or FM or anything. There were four small dials, one at each point of the glass triangle and one at the bottom center with a metal switch.

I tested the dials. Two of them moved the needles in the faceplate. The other one didn't do anything. I turned the metal switch back and forth a couple of times, but nothing happened. When I stepped back, I noticed the electric cord lying on top of a box—it wasn't plugged in.

I moved the boxes out of the way, kicking up a cloud of dust that made the place feel even creepier than it already was. I pushed the radio closer to the wall and plugged it in. For a quick moment, I got that feeling again, as if I'd lived this moment before.

I turned the switch on, but nothing happened. I shook the stupid cabinet back and forth, slapped the top with the palm of my hand a couple of times, but all it did was hiss for a couple seconds, then fall quiet. I checked behind it. The whole back was open. It had a metal platform like a box with a bunch of wires and strange-looking parts and six small glass bulbs stamped with the same Zenith logo that was on the faceplate. The little bulbs were flickering on and off like they were struggling to turn on but couldn't. One of the bulbs came on, then turned off completely. I tried unscrewing it, but it wouldn't turn. I stepped back and stared at the stupid thing. Nothing ever worked for me—the PS3, the binoculars, my brain. I kicked the cabinet, and walked away, and then came back and switched it off.

I walked to the front of the room and was about to walk out, but I got that weird feeling again, as if I had been here before. I didn't know why it kept happening, but it was starting to freak me out, like maybe something was wrong with me. I paced back and forth a couple of times trying to remember, trying to figure out this feeling. I don't know. Maybe it was something I had to do, otherwise it would be like Hugo winning all over again. But I marched back and turned the radio back on. The bulbs were lighting up, but real weak, just tiny orange sparks. Except for the one that didn't light up. I grabbed it and tried turning it. When it didn't come off, I pulled it and—*zap!*

A huge blue spark zapped like lightning—scared the crap out of me. The bulb wasn't like a regular light bulb. It had these metal prongs at the bottom, and the inside had all this grayish stuff. I shook it next to my ear but didn't hear if anything was loose or broken. It took me a few tries to reconnect it to the radio. When I finally got it plugged in, it sparked a couple of times, then it lit up like the others. A speaker in the bottom part of the cabinet made a loud buzz, then crackled and hissed low and deep. But there was no music. Behind the radio, the glass of the picture of the ocean reflected the lights from the little bulbs in the back of the radio, six tiny orange lights against the dark storm clouds.

Little by little, the glass faceplate glowed, first orange and yellow, then it got brighter. I turned the dial, moving the needle in a circle trying to find a station, but I couldn't get a signal. The hissing went on, sounded like a truck engine idling. Then the faceplate flashed, filling the room with light, then went dark.

My anger faded. The thing that had been choking me for I don't know how long finally let go. The squiggly feeling in my stomach, the confusion vanished. Despite the dust and the stink, I took a deep breath in. I could breathe. It was as if a strong breeze had swept past and taken all the bad away. Kind of like when I sat with Lupe on the roof. And for the first time since forever, I felt as if everything was okay, as if I was a regular person with regular memories like everyone else. It even felt as if my father was there with me.

When I walked out of the closet, it was dark outside, which was strange because I was sure I'd only been in the room for like twenty minutes.

21.

The next morning, Ma was rushing around in the kitchen, dressed in her scrubs—purple pants and a loose shirt with a bunch of colored hearts that looked like a kid had drawn them with crayons. She had her hair up in a bun, no makeup or jewelry, a cloth face mask and an ID badge hanging around her neck.

"What happened to your other mask?" I said.

"We're out of N95s again. I'm going to have to wear this over a surgical mask. And my face shield on top of that." She stopped and took a long drink of coffee, then made her way around the counter. "Have you seen my keys?"

"How come?"

My arm was sore and my knees scraped. But my anger from the encounter with Hugo had faded. Instead, I had this weird memory that wasn't really a memory—or maybe it was. All I saw was the image of a skeleton woman and a house with an orange floor.

Ma paused and looked at me. "What?"

"Why do you have to wear two masks and we only wear one?"

"I need the extra protection, mi amor. I work with Covid patients. You don't."

"Why's the clinic out of N95s?"

"Lalo . . ."

I followed her to the living room. "Did we ever live in a house with an orange floor?"

"An orange floor?" She pulled away the couch cushions one by one. "Where the—"

"I think I might have a memory. I was sitting on an orange floor. I think Papi was there."

"Ay, Lalo, please. Help me find my keys."

"Did you check your purse?"

Her mouth twisted to the side in an exaggerated smirk. "What do you think?"

"There was a couch and a blue window. And a skeleton woman."

"I have no idea what you're talking about, mi amor."

"I think she was a doll." I followed her into her bedroom. "She had this big hat with flowers, and her head wobbled."

"Sounds like la Catrina." She placed her hands on her waist. "Where. Are. My. Keys?"

"Did we ever have one of those?"

"I don't know, maybe."

"I think it's a memory," I said. "But it could've been a dream. Because I also remember Papi. Well, I don't really remember him. I just have this feeling that he was telling me I should be proud of who I am. I think he meant for being Haitian."

"Absolutely, you should." Her eyes darted around the room

as she spoke. "Your father was a very proud man. He used to say, 'Haiti might be poor, but it's free.' Haiti had the only successful slave rebellion. And they helped Simón Bolívar win Colombian independence. Tell that to Irma." She raised her chin and smiled. "That's why your father was so confident. He used to say that if his ancestors could fight Napoleon's army and the British and Spanish armies—and win—he knew in his heart that he could do anything he set his mind to."

"What about the orange floor and the blue window?"

"Ay, I don't know," she cried, and peeked in the bathroom. "I'm going to be late for work."

"Maybe Claudio took them."

She rushed into our room. But Claudio wasn't home. She gave the kitchen another quick look, then walked out the front door and stopped. Her keys were hanging on the deadbolt.

"Dios mío," she cried. "Where's my head?"

"You think it's a memory or a dream?"

"What?" She paused for a moment, her arms loaded with her purse, cup of coffee, a plastic bag with a sour cream container with leftover rice and beans, a bottle of water, and her keys.

"The house and the Catrina and Papi?"

"What house, mi amor?"

"I just told you. The house with the orange floor and the blue window—"

"Ay, Lalo, I don't know. I don't remember." She leaned over and kissed my forehead. "I'm running late. Please do your homework."

She stepped out and closed the door.

I thought of the skeleton woman, tried to remember. So much seemed to hang on the tip of my tongue, but I couldn't figure out what it was, what it meant.

Then Ma marched back in. "Yes, Lalo. I'm sorry." Her eyes were wide, excited. "The house. It was our house. But the floor wasn't orange, it was tile, terra-cotta tile."

"What about the skeleton woman?"

"La Catrina. Maybe. I can't remember. But I don't see why not." She gave me a tight hug and a kiss on the cheek. Her eyes welled up.

"It could've been a dream," I said.

"A memory, a dream. It doesn't matter." She wiped her eyes with the heel of her hand, the plastic bag with her lunch looped around her fingers. "It was a beautiful house with Saltillo tile and big windows."

"Blue?"

"No, not blue," she said. "It's the first time you have a memory from that house, Lalo."

"Other than puff-puff."

"Yes!" She smiled, showing her big teeth. "I have to run, mi amor. Be good."

I went out to the walkway and watched her get in her car and drive away. I kept looking at the parking lot, but I didn't really see the parking lot. I saw orange tile, the Catrina doll with her sunken eyes and smiling face and the colorful flowers on her giant hat. I saw cardboard boxes on the floor and the kitchen counter. And I heard Papi's deep voice saying something about a cat.

22.

I knew Claudio didn't tell Ma I was up on the roof, otherwise she would've killed me. And Claudio would've gotten in trouble, too. He probably knew Ma would get the details out of me—about how they'd bullied Vivi and me. That's the thing with Ma. If she found out one thing, she found out everything. Once, she punished Claudio for his grades, but report cards weren't even out yet. And before we went on lockdown, she grounded him for sleeping in class—she wasn't even there. It's like she had spies or radar or something.

I went upstairs to see Vivi. But when she opened the door, she just stood there, half her face covered by one of Alita's embroidered masks, her narrow brown eyes staring at me like she didn't know who I was.

"What?"

She crossed her arms and shifted her weight on one leg. "*What* what?"

I showed her the binoculars. "We're spying on Robachico, no?"

"You for real, o qué?"

It was as if I was facing the Vivi from before lockdown, the one who didn't talk to me, even on the school bus.

"You don't remember?"

"About Hugo and Claudio?" I said.

"That's not what I'm talking about."

"Then what?"

She told me what happened, how I went totally nuts on Hugo and then on her after we got downstairs. "You acted like a— Like bien menso."

"I'm sorry." I didn't remember any of it, but I was sure it happened like she said. I was a time bomb. I knew I could lose it in a big way. And then forget anything ever happened.

"Apologies are a sign of abusive behavior," she said.

"What are you talking about?"

"You shouldn't have to apologize, Lalo."

"Wait, what?"

"If you didn't act like a jerk," she said, "you wouldn't have to apologize."

"But I am sorry. It's just . . . sometimes I feel like there's all this stuff going on in my head. Like a bunch of noise. And then I have this thing that presses against me like a big rock, like that Tlaloc statue Alita showed us. And what Hugo said about my father and how he had me like that and I couldn't move. I saw your face and Claudio and Jesse laughing . . . I don't know. I lost it. And when you were telling me to chill, it was as if you were taking their side. I don't want to be treated like baby or like I'm—"

"Listen." She stopped me, the palm of her hand up to my face. "I don't take crap from anyone. ¿Entiendes?"

I wasn't one hundred percent sure what she meant by abusive. As far as I was concerned, Claudio and Hugo were the abusive ones. And sometimes, even Vivi could be like that—bossy and demanding and annoying. But she was my friend. She could say whatever she wanted about our relationship, but it was true. We were friends. And I cared about her. I didn't want to imagine what the lockdown would be like if we didn't hang out.

"I have a surprise," I said, and put out my fist for her to tap. "Peace?"

She stared at my hand, at me, at my hand. I could tell a smile was growing under her mask. "Fine." She tapped my fist with hers. "Peace."

"Promise you won't tell anyone."

We ran downstairs and to the back of the building. When I reached the door, Vivi stopped and placed her hands on the sides of her waist. "Pallets?"

"Check it out." I pulled the door open.

We walked inside, turned the light on. "It's a storage closet full of vintage stuff."

"It stinks like wet socks." She pinched her nose and nodded at the boxes. "Whose stuff is this?"

"No idea." Then I pointed to the bicycle with the cooler. "That's Don Frank's."

She leaned over a broken bicycle and grabbed a small pink box. "Postcards," she whispered, and leafed through the pictures. "Lisbon, Madrid, Jamaica . . . There's no writing on them."

I looked over her shoulder at the cards. "Weird. You think someone went to all these places?"

"It's a collection."

"I wonder if the people with the same postcards have the same memories."

"They can't." She set the postcards back in the box. "Everyone's memories are different. Alita says two people can remember the same moment differently."

"How do they do that?"

"I don't know. It's perception or perspective. Whatever. It's just how it is."

I tapped the top of the wooden radio. "Check this out."

"What is it?"

"I'm pretty sure it's an old-time radio."

She ran her hand over the glass faceplate. "Does it work?"

"Kind of."

"Looks like something Alita would listen to."

"I'm pretty sure it's older than Alita."

"Hey!" She moved to the other side of the radio and tapped the keys of the typewriter that was sitting on top of the big clothes dryer. "It works."

"It's strange how this stuff mattered once and now it's useless."

"It's not useless." Vivi tapped on the typewriter a few times, then she opened the black case sitting on one of the boxes and pulled out a small movie camera.

"Lalo, check it out." She put the camera up to her eye and pointed the lens at me. "Wave or do something."

I waved and turned back to the radio.

"Maybe we can make a documentary of how boring life is

in the lockdown," she said, and panned around the room. She set the camera down next to the typewriter and opened the front of the dryer and peeked inside. "Smells like laundry soap."

I went back to the radio and turned it on.

"Lalo, look." Vivi crawled into the dryer. "It's a space capsule." She closed the door and waved at me, her body curled up in a ball.

I turned the switch on the radio. The bulbs in the back flickered, reflecting against the glass of the framed picture of the ocean. It looked like a sunset. The hissing started, first low, then louder. The faceplate lit up, first a deep yellow, then brighter. I turned the dial to see if I could find some music.

"I think it needs an antenna," I said.

Vivi didn't answer.

I kept turning the dial back and forth, trying to get a station. The faceplate lit up brighter and brighter. Then it flashed, filling the closet with light, and I saw the house with the orange floor, except I couldn't be sure because I was looking up at my mom. She was younger and holding a cat in her arms. She was talking to someone I couldn't see, maybe my father. Claudio came in carrying a box. He set it on the kitchen counter and walked back outside.

When I turned the radio off, the hissing sound kept ringing in my ears. Then I heard a knock at the far end of the room.

"Vivi?"

Knock—knock-knock.

"Vivi?"

"Lalo!" Her voice was muffled, followed by knocking and banging. "Help me!"

"Vivi!"

"Help!"

It sounded as if she was screaming but someone was covering her mouth. I thought of Robachico. "Vivi!" My heart pounded hard against my ribs. "Vivi!"

I jumped over the broken microwave. Vivi. She was curled up inside the dryer, waving and banging on the plexiglass door with the palm of her hand.

"Lalo!"

She had her mask off. Her face was twisted, eyes wide. Her mouth moved, but I couldn't make out what she was saying.

"What's wrong?"

"Open the door." She hammered the door with the palm of her hand. "Get me out!"

I pulled the door handle, but it wouldn't open.

"Lemme out!" she cried, and banged her hand frantically against the door. I pulled with both hands, put all my weight into it. But it wouldn't move.

"Get me out!"

I stepped back and studied the dryer.

Vivi pressed her face against the plexiglass. "Help me. Get me out!"

There was a small lever next to the slot for the quarters. I turned it and the door swung open. Vivi slid out like she was made of liquid and sat on the floor.

"What the hell?" she cried.

"What happened?"

She pulled herself up. "What is wrong with you?"

"What are you talking about?"

"I was in there forever," she yelled, pushed me out of the way and stormed out of the closet.

"We haven't even been here for ten minutes!"

"No!" she cried. "You— You did it on purpose!"

Outside, the sky was a deep blue. The sharp light of the sun cut across the alley from the west. Vivi was right. We'd been in the closet for way more than ten minutes.

23.

That night I couldn't fall asleep. Every time I closed my eyes, I saw the panic in Vivi's face. It was scary. But I also had this weird dream-like feeling, as if I was here in my room, on the bed, but wasn't. I stared at the ceiling, my eyes tracing the cracks in the paint like roads on a map taking me to a million different memories I knew nothing about. But one cloudy memory did float over me long enough for me to remember. Mexican music playing, a DJ was speaking Spanish. Papi was there. I couldn't see him, but the more I thought about it, I began to understand the memory—a treasure, something about Haiti and a treasure full of gold.

I sat up. Claudio was lying on his bed facing the wall, earbuds in. "Claudio . . ."

He didn't move.

"Claudio?" I threw my pillow at him.

He turned over and yanked his earbuds out. "What's your problem, fool?"

"I was calling you."

He tapped his phone a couple of times and tossed me my pillow. "Can't you see I'm watching something?"

"Do you remember Papi telling us about a treasure?"

"Whatchoo talking about?"

"When we were little," I said. "We were at a party or something and Papi told us a story about how he found a treasure in Haiti?"

"That was just a story. He was trying to make a point."

"What was the point?"

Claudio sighed. "It was about how a friend or someone he knew found a pot of gold coins from when Haiti was part of France or something. He became rich but was unhappy and died alone."

"It wasn't Papi?"

"We weren't rich, fool. Papi worked. He left Haiti to work in the Dominican Republic when he was a kid younger than you. Then he came here and worked his way through school, did all that on his own."

"I don't remember that."

"We weren't born then, fool."

"What did he do?"

"He was an X-ray technician, worked for a radiologist at one of the big hospitals, Lee Memorial or the other one, I'm not sure."

"Radiologist," I whispered to myself. "Does that have anything to do with radios?"

"X-rays," he said, and put the earbuds back in. "That's how he met Ma." He tapped his phone a couple of times and leaned back on his pillow.

LALO LESPÉRANCE NEVER FORGOT

"Claudio."

He glanced up.

"Do you tell people you're Haitian?"

"Why you ask me that?"

"It's just"—I turned away for a second—"people always think I'm Cuban or Dominican. They don't believe I'm Mexican because I look more Black than Mexican."

"To hell with 'em."

"Sometimes I don't know what I am. Like without Papi here, I don't feel Haitian. Does that happen to you?"

"Nope."

"You don't use your Haitian name."

"So?"

"So, you have Papi's name and you changed it."

He pulled his earbuds out again. I thought he was going to throw something at me, but he just stared at me for a moment. Then he said, "It's easier like that."

"Did he talk Spanish?"

"What kind of a stupid question is that? Of course he did."

I glanced at my hands, my fingers laced together on my lap. They reminded me of my father even though I couldn't actually remember holding his hand. "I don't like to say I'm Haitian 'cause people make fun of it. Even the Haitians laugh because I don't speak Creole. It's as if I don't belong here or there."

"Just say you're Mexican."

"But it feels wrong. Like . . . like I'm erasing Papi."

"Listen," he said, "forget Haiti."

"But—"

"*Forget it.* Papi's dead. That's where Haiti ends for us. For me and for you."

"But people are always asking where I'm from and—"

"Just say you're Mexican. It's easier." Claudio turned over, but then he glanced at me real quick before putting in his earbuds. "The only people who don't have to explain themselves are white."

24.

The following morning Vivi wouldn't talk to me—not a word, didn't even look at me. She turned the page of her history book and highlighted something, focused on what the teacher was saying, and went about her day as if I didn't exist.

The uncomfortable tightness in my stomach came back with a vengeance. I had to keep running to the bathroom. They were mostly false alarms, but I did have a little diarrhea a couple of times. It went on like that all day. I was sure it had to do with Vivi or with my dreams. I couldn't remember them, but it was as if the world had changed. Or maybe I was just in a strange mood. I kept thinking about what Claudio had said. But I didn't agree with him. Just because Papi was no longer with us, it didn't mean we should forget our Haitian side. The problem was, I knew nothing about Haiti except poverty, earthquakes, and hurricanes. I had no idea what it was like to be Haitian. I didn't even speak the language. So how could I even claim to be Haitian?

Tortillas frying in the kitchen saved me from my thoughts. That smell of corn and oil took me back to the first time I ate quesadillas at Vivi's house. They were so good, a million times better than the ones Ma made. Alita used dark corn tortillas and queso Oaxaca she got at the store where they sell Mexican stuff. She fried them so the edges were nice and crispy, and the cheese melted like when you get pizza at a restaurant. That time, Alita served them with this super-spicy green salsa, and Vivi made fun of me because I had to drink like ten glasses of water to stop my mouth from burning.

I remembered! I wasn't even trying and I remembered. Every little detail came back to me like a movie—I ate three quesadillas, Alita offered to make a milder salsa for me, Claudio kept coughing but couldn't stop eating, the glass I drank from had a Scooby-Doo cartoon on it, and the ice cubes had melted together making the shape of a heart, but when I showed Vivi she said it looked more like a butt and we laughed.

I wanted to scream. But I couldn't. No one would care—not Vivi or Claudio. Maybe Alita would. And Ma. She'd be thrilled. I wrote a note on my hand to tell Ma I remembered the quesadillas at Vivi's.

When I was in second grade, Ma took me to all kinds of doctors to see why I forgot things. They gave me tests and asked questions, they even put me in a machine that scanned my brain, but no one could figure out what was going on. One doctor said it had to do with when I was sick with asthma, that the lack of oxygen affected the part of my brain where memories were stored. Another said it could be from the lead paint at our old apartment. The school counselor was sure it was a form of ADHD or selective amnesia from trauma. She said something

I'd seen or done had affected me in a way that shocked my brain into forgetting as a defense mechanism to shield me from the pain. But since I couldn't remember, there was no way to tell what that was.

The moment class was over, Vivi closed the laptop and marched into her room—didn't say a word to me.

I shoved my schoolbooks into my backpack and was about to walk out when Alita stopped me. "A ver, mijo, tell me what's going on. No quiero ser metiche. But it pains my heart to see you and Viviana not getting along."

I glanced at the bag of masks she'd made. I was about to tell her about Vivi getting stuck in the clothes dryer when Lupe stormed out of her room.

"¿Adónde vas?" Alita demanded.

"Out." Lupe glanced at me. It was just for a millisecond, but in that tiny moment it felt as if she were greeting me, saying, *What's up, Lalo,* and then glancing at Alita again with this expression as if she'd tasted something horrible and wanted to spit it out.

Alita removed her reading glasses. "I asked you where."

"To get some air."

"Tu mamá doesn't want you out in the street, eh?"

"I know." Lupe rolled her eyes. And somehow I knew she was going up to the roof, where she felt free. I got it one hundred percent because I wanted that, too. We all wanted that feeling. Except freedom for me was different from freedom for Lupe.

"The parking lot is not the street," she added, and glanced at me real quick but this time without any intention, just a blank

stare that said nothing. That was her look, the one with the attitude that couldn't care less about anyone or anything—the one
that gave her the reputation of being mean and a psycho. Then
she walked out, slamming the door behind her.

"Esa niña." Alita shook her head and set her embroidery
aside. "She was trouble before el lockdown. And now? I worry
about her state of mind. Siempre solita, la pobre—always alone.
And with such an attitude. No sé que le pasa. It's not healthy."

"I'm sure she's fine."

"No sé, Lalo. When I was her age, I was always busy. I helped
my parents with the house. I played volleyball at school and was
learning to sew, I had friends."

I sat next to Alita. "She's not you."

"She's very desconectada. It's as if she hates everything. And
el lockdown is not helping."

"Maybe you should accept her for who she is."

"No, I don't understand her." She shook her head, and
her eyes seemed to search for something in my face. "But tell
me . . ." She squinted slightly, the wrinkles in the sides of her
eyes stretched. "¿Y tú? How are you, mijo?"

There was so much I wanted to tell her, but I didn't know
where to start. She caressed my head, the palm of her hand glid-
ing gently over my hair. It usually annoyed me when people did
that, but not Alita. With her, it wasn't because I had a messy
Afro or because she was feeling sorry for me. It was just nice.

"You know how sometimes I can't remember stuff?" I leaned
to the side and adjusted my mask. "I think I'm starting to remember, just little bits, but it's something, right?"

"Qué bien. Sí, this is very good, Lalo. Poquito a poquito se llena el jarrito—little by little. I am sure you will soon remember everything."

"I was wondering . . . like . . . do you think maybe there is some special Mexican magic or maybe one of those healers you talked about who could help me?"

"¿La curandera?" she said with a sigh. "No sé, Lalo. I don't know of any in this country, and we would have to find the right one. It might take a lot of work. Back home we would have it much easier. You just ask and people know. They tell you where to go."

"But it is possible, right?"

"Supongo que sí," she said. "There was a woman on the south side of my neighborhood who cured my cousin of delusions of the future."

I stared at her hands. The wrinkles and veins and spots held stories and secrets like the pages in a book. I realized then that even though she shared her stories with me, I would never know her whole life and her joys and her suffering. Maybe that was the thing—we all suffered from something and only we knew it. We all have problems that make us who we are. Alita suffered from nostalgia; her cousin suffered from the future. I suffered from the past. But for the first time in forever, I had hope. I was starting to remember.

"Do you ever wish you could go back in time?"

She laughed. "All the time, mijo. All the time."

"I'd like to go back and see my father."

Alita turned to face the bureau with the photos.

"Is it José?" I said.

She shook her head. "I was only thinking . . ."

"How come you can see him, but I can't see my father?"

She set her hand on my knee and explained how there were things I needed to work on. "Además, have you ever put out an ofrenda for him on the Day of the Dead?"

"I don't think so."

"Well, that would be a good start. Come the last week in October, I will help you. We'll go to the mercado and get strings of Cempasúchil flowers and pan de muerto, quizá a few sugar skulls, and we'll put out some photographs and his favorite goodies, cosas que le gustaban."

"But he wasn't Mexican," I said.

"No importa." She waved her hand as if she was shooing a fly. "He will know you are inviting him. We will make a very beautiful offering so he will know he is welcome. Los Haitianos have their own Day of the Dead. They believe in spirits the same way we do in Mexico, only our rituals are a little different. But trust me, the intention is the same. And in the end, down here"—she tapped the middle of my chest—"we're all very much alike."

"And I'll be able to see him and talk to him?"

"Claro que sí." She leaned her head to the side and winked. "I do it all the time."

25.

When I went home to drop off my backpack, I found a box on my dresser. The soldering kit—with a note: *Do not solder inside the house and wear your goggles, love you.* It was from Ma, as if I didn't know about safety. I ran into her room to thank her, but she wasn't there. I guess that explained the note.

Back in my room, I searched the drawers for my swimming goggles. Then I grabbed the parts of the PS3 and laid everything out on the living room floor. I checked my notes from my science teacher and followed the diagram I had drawn out in my notebook. There was no way I could work outside because there were no outlets on the walkway. So I opened the windows in the living room and turned on the ceiling fan. I plugged in the soldering iron. I put on the goggles and got to work putting the circuits and transistors back in what I hoped were the right places.

But soldering wasn't as easy as it looked in the YouTube videos I studied at school before the lockdown. They made soldering seem so simple. You heat a coil of solder wire so it melts and drips where you're connecting a wire. But every time I melted the coil with the iron, the solder dripped on the wrong places. I ended up with a mess of solder points on the motherboard.

I did manage to attach a few parts, but I still needed three long wires to connect the machine to the electrodes I was going to attach to my brain.

I set the PS3 on the coffee table and ran downstairs. I figured I could pull some wires from one of the old appliances in the storage closet. But as I came around to the back of the building, I saw a beat-up old car with no bumper and a broken headlight parked right in front of the door to the storage closet. Two skinny legs stuck out from under the front of the car—Socrates. He cursed, said something about his mother, then crawled out from under the car. He sat there, no mask, and stared at his finger for a moment. Then he looked at me. "¿Qué pasa, chico?"

"What are you doing?"

He kissed his finger and winced. "Almost chopped my finger off trying to loosen the water pump on this beast."

"Yeah, but— But why are you here?"

He looked left and right. "¿Qué? What's wrong with this place?"

"It's just . . . you always work in the parking lot."

He stood and pulled up his shorts, which were hanging below his bony hips. "I just got it. Beautiful, eh? It's a classic." He petted the hood of the car. "I used to have one just like it in Cuba. But Nazario says he don't want it sitting in the parking lot. Says it's an eyesore. He lets that RV park out there for months like it's the Taj Mahal, but this beauty? Por favor, chico. It's an injustice."

The car was big with curved front fenders and rear end, faded green paint with patches of gray and orange rust. Vivi would call it vintage. But the problem was that it was parked by the door to the storage closet. I couldn't let Socrates see me go in there. If he didn't stop me, he'd for sure tell Nazario. They'd put a lock on it. "So, you're just going to leave it here?"

"Sí, claro. Until I get it running." He raised the hood and leaned in, half his body over the engine bay so it looked as if the car might swallow him bones and all.

I wandered slowly up the stairs. All I needed was three long wires. For a moment, I considered going home and spying on Robachico, but Vivi had the binoculars. Besides, she wasn't talking to me, and spying on Robachico was only fun when I was with Vivi.

I went up to the roof instead. I wanted to think. I sat on the front facing the parking lot, pulled my mask off, and took a few deep breaths. Just three wires. That and three Band-Aids to attach the wires to my brain. Then, if the machine worked, I would see my memories. The plan kept swirling in my head, searching for any loose ends. I could see the finished product. I imagined my brain and the deep places where memories were stored. I didn't see it like Vivi—that it would also mean I'd be going back in time. The PS3 was only going to take out what was hidden in my neocortex and store it in a video. It wasn't rocket science. I was sure it was going to work.

A black bird flew past and seemed to float in the air, level with me. The way it glided about twenty yards away made me smile. I was sure it was checking me out. Made me think of the moths and butterflies and Alita's stories about spirits. I wondered if it meant anything. I had to tell Alita.

I was glad to know you didn't have to be one hundred percent Mexican for the spirits and magic to work. Day of the Dead was still months away, but I was already planning it out in my head, thinking of Papi's favorite things and how I would make a huge ofrenda with Alita's help. I told myself to make a list of questions to ask Papi's spirit when he came. There was so much I wanted to know about him and Haiti. Then I could tell people I was Haitian with all the pride in my heart.

"What're you doing here?" Lupe walked onto the roof, black jeans, a black T-shirt with the sleeves cut off and a design like the seal of the United States that said RAMONES, a black hoodie tied around her waist. Her hair was up in a ponytail. My eyes traced the line of her jaw, high cheekbones, and lips that I swear were fighting back a smile.

"No mask?" I said.

"What about you?" She stopped a few feet away from where I was.

I put my mask on.

"Don't worry." She sat cross-legged where she stood. "That's why I like it here. No mask. Feels like before Covid."

"Me too," I said. "Except now Claudio and Hugo discovered it."

"What's the deal with those guys anyway?"

"Vivi calls them huevones."

She chuckled. "Sounds about right."

I looked at the parking lot.

"So, are you and Vivi like boyfriend and girlfriend or what?"

"No!"

"Makes sense," she said with a nod.

"What?"

"The lockdown. She doesn't know how to be alone. You're friends of convenience."

I hated hearing it, but it was true. "What about you?"

She tilted her head to the side. The sunlight cut across her pretty face, made her eyes shine. "Isn't it obvious?"

I had no idea what she meant by that, probably just Lupe trying to be mysterious. "Why are you so mean to Alita?"

"What's it to you?"

"Never mind," I said.

She glanced down at her silver bracelet for a moment. The lines she had drawn on her hand were barely noticeable. "I despise authority, if you must know."

"What does that even mean?"

"I love my grandmother, okay?" She placed her hand on her chest. "I really do. I just don't like being told what to do all the time."

I felt the same way, especially when Claudio ordered me around as if he were my father. "Vivi's not talking to me anymore."

"I know." She stretched her leg out from under her. She was wearing black combat boots. "She complains about you all the time."

"What?"

"You know, that you forget important stuff. She says it's frustrating."

"How do you think it makes me feel?"

"Dude, I'm just telling you what she said. It's not me."

"Whatever," I said. "But that's not why she's not talking to me."

"She said you locked her in one of the dryers."

"That's a lie. She locked herself in."

"Right, she would do something like that, too." She laughed. "But don't worry, she'll get over it. Vivi has this tendency to make a big deal out of nothing. I think it's what happens when you're the youngest."

"I'm the youngest."

"I see." She tilted her head down and raised her eyes, grinned mischievously. "And are you a big drama queen or what?"

I laughed. "I don't know . . . maybe."

"So, guess what?" She nodded. "I broke up with my boyfriend."

"Why?"

"He's dull."

"You mean boring?"

"Same thing." She stood and turned to face the back of the building. "You think I can jump across the alley and reach the light pole?"

There was an electric pole across the alley opposite our building, like twenty or thirty feet from the edge. "No way."

"I bet I could parkour from the roof to the pole and land on the top of the dumpster."

"That's impossible. Besides, it's too low." I followed her to the back of the roof. We stood side by side at the edge, looking down. Socrates's car was directly below us.

Lupe squinted at the pole, measuring the distance. "Yeah, I can do it." She pointed at each part. "Pole. Dumpster. Car. Ground. Easy."

"No. You'll die."

"We're all gonna die sometime."

"Even if you make it across, there's nothing to hold on to. And if you touch a wire, you'll get electrocuted."

She walked backward to the middle of the roof, eyes fixed ahead to where the pole was. "I'm gonna do it."

"Lupe—"

She grinned and leaned forward, ready to sprint.

"Don't joke around."

"Who's joking?" She ran.

I blocked her path. "No!"

I grabbed her and pulled her back, my hand holding her arm until she came around in a circle, and we froze in a hug, our faces inches away, staring into each other's eyes. "God, Lalo." She pushed me away and walked backward toward the secret stairs. "You're no fun."

26.

A little while later, I went back to the storage closet to find wires for my memory machine. Socrates's car sat in the same place like a metal sculpture, but he wasn't there.

I hurried inside and scanned the room for electric appliances. No way was I going to mess up the radio. But the microwave . . . I turned it over on its side, but the back was sealed with screws. I considered running home and getting a screwdriver or just smashing the stupid thing, but the radio caught my eye. It sat there as if it was waiting for me. I went over and turned it on. The bulbs lit up slowly, orange and blue dots reflecting against the glass of the picture of the ocean. The speaker buzzed lightly, then fell into that deep hiss. A moment later the faceplate lit up yellow, flickered a couple of times, and flashed, filling the room with light.

I saw myself sitting at the kitchen counter of a house I didn't recognize. I was five years old. Claudio was probably ten. Ma was there, too. There were cardboard boxes on the orange floor. Terra-cotta tiles.

Ma set her purse on the counter and rubbed her temples.

Her hair was a mess. She looked serious, angry, eyes red and dark all around like she'd been crying.

Claudio disappeared into a room. Ma followed him. Something was wrong, but I couldn't tell what it was. Five-year-old me didn't know what was going on, ignored them, stirred chocolate powder into a glass of milk.

"Don't . . ." Ma was upset at Claudio. "You understand me? Just don't."

Claudio cried, "If he hadn't been such a—"

"I'm asking you, Claudio. Por favor," Ma said.

"But why—"

"He doesn't understand," she said.

"But if he—"

"What if it had been you?" Ma said. "What then?"

"But it wasn't me. It was his fault—"

"Por el amor de Dios," Ma cried, her voice tearing through the house. "I don't want to hear another word about it! Ever!"

The house fell silent except for the tinny sound of the spoon against the glass as five-year-old me stirred the chocolate milk. When little me drank, I could taste the chocolate as if I was drinking it now.

Then Claudio yelled, "I hate him!"

Five-year-old me winced at the sound of Ma slapping Claudio. A moment later, Ma said, "You don't. You're just angry. You love your brother—"

"What about Papi?"

"Enough," Ma cried. "I don't want to hear another word about this, you understand?"

The door to the room flew open, and Ma marched out. She glanced at five-year-old me, then disappeared into another room and shut the door.

Claudio stepped out and stood at the threshold, stared at five-year-old me for a long time. The hate in his eyes made the back of my neck tingle. But five-year-old me didn't get it. He just sat there, stirring his chocolate milk.

I wanted to say something, but it was like a dream. All I could do was see and hear—and taste. I was there but I wasn't there.

Claudio stepped back in the room and shut the door. Five-year-old me looked across the house at the big window in the living room. Then he lowered his head and for the longest time just sat there alone.

I opened my mouth to speak, but nothing would come out.

When five-year-old me raised his head, his eyes were red, cheeks moist with tears. He sniffled a couple of times and wiped his eyes with the back of his hand.

I tried to speak. I wanted to say it was going to be fine. I tried again and again but nothing would come out of my mouth, not a sound. And five-year-old me just sat there weeping in the kitchen—alone.

Finally, I heard my voice. "Okay."

The moment the word came out of my mouth, I saw the front of the radio glowing softly. I was back in the closet. I turned the radio off and sat on the broken microwave and stared down at my sneakers. What I saw must have been a memory, it had to be. It swirled in my head like a bunch of movie clips—Ma slapping Claudio—yelling—door slamming—five-year-old me crying. But Claudio's hate was so real. The whole scene went around and around, repeating itself, but it always ended with him yelling, saying he hated me, and then the sound of Ma slapping him. And worse, Claudio didn't even cry. The whole thing squeezed my stomach like a sponge. A tightness in my throat rose to where I couldn't stop it, and I dropped my head in my hands and cried.

27.

The next day during class I kept thinking of what happened in the storage closet. I kept telling myself it was a memory, but what I saw was too real—more real than a dream. I was there. I tasted the chocolate milk. But even more weird was how the emotions from that moment had transferred from five-year-old me to my current self. Even now, I had this lingering sadness that wouldn't go away. Maybe something about that radio was magic. No one talked about American magic, but it probably existed. Maybe the radio had somehow tuned into my past as if it were a radio station and played my memories.

I couldn't tell Vivi about it. I wanted to, but she was still not talking to me. Besides, she would probably make fun of me. I couldn't ask Ma because she wasn't coming home for another couple of days. And asking Claudio why he was mad at me six years ago would be totally useless. I could already hear him, "Whatchoo talking about, fool?"

Our last class was science. I wanted to ask Mr. Z about the radio, but we were studying volcanoes, how there are different types all over the world. He showed us pictures of the eruptions of the Soufrière volcano on the island of Montserrat, which covered everything in lava and ash, and we saw these super-creepy pictures that showed how the eruption of Mount Vesuvius in AD 79 that killed a ton of people in Pompeii left the people frozen in a moment in time like statues.

About five minutes before class ended, Alita sat at our table and closed the computer.

"Alita!" Vivi cried. "You can't do that."

"What does that man know about volcanoes?" she said.

"He's a teacher." Vivi opened the laptop, but we'd lost the Zoom connection. Mr. Z was frozen in the window, eyes half closed, mouth open. "He's a nerd, but he knows what he's talking about," Vivi went on, clicking on the link, trying to reconnect us. "Probably read the textbook a million times."

"Ese no sabe nada," Alita said with a wave of her hand. "Did he bother to mention that the most beautiful volcanoes in the world are in Mexico?"

"Seriously?" I said.

"Claro, Popocatépetl e Iztaccíhuatl."

"Popo-what?" I laughed.

Alita pushed the computer aside. "El Popo y el Izta."

"Oh God." Vivi leaned to the side and whispered her first words to me since she ran out of the storage closet the other day: "It's another one of her loco stories."

"Sí, Viviana. It is one of my stories," Alita said firmly. "But it is also your story. And yours too, Lalo."

Vivi rolled her eyes. "Here we go."

Alita ignored her and started with the story about Popocatépetl and how he was a brave and handsome Tlaxcalteca warrior.

"You mean Aztec," Vivi corrected her.

"No, niña. Tlaxcalteca. They were the enemies of the Aztecs."

"Okay, if you say so," Vivi said sarcastically.

"The Aztecs weren't the only people in Mexico," Alita explained. "But allow me to me continue with the story, por favor. Iztaccíhuatl was a beautiful princess, and Popo, the handsome warrior, was in love with her. So, he went to see her father, a great Tlaxcalteca cacique, and—"

I raised my hand. "What's a cacique?"

"A cacique is the most important chief of a tribe," Alita said, and went on about how Popo asked for Izta's hand in marriage from the cacique. "But the timing was not good. The Tlaxcaltecas were about to go to battle against the Aztecs. So, the cacique promised Popo that when he came home safe from the battle, he could marry Izta. But while Popo was away fighting the Aztecs, a jealous warrior who wanted Izta for himself told her that Popo had been killed in battle. Claro, era mentira—a lie—but Izta believed him and the poor girl died of heartbreak."

"You can't die of heartbreak," Vivi said. "It's scientifically impossible."

"Let her tell the story," I said.

"Pues entonces, poor Popo returned from battle only to find that his beloved Izta had died. His love for Izta was so deep, he ordered that a huge mountain be made from ten mountains so he could lay Izta to rest close to the sun."

"Impossible," Vivi said flatly.

"It's possible," I said. "Mexican magic, right, Alita?"

"Ten mountains?" Vivi said. "How could they even—"

"Por favor, niños." Alita tapped the table with her knuckles. "Let me finish." She cleared her throat and accommodated her mask that was starting to slide down her nose. "Entonces, the Tlaxcaltecas made this huge mountain where Popo laid Izta to rest. Popo sat beside her to keep her company forever, holding an eternal torch. That, niños, is how the volcanos Popocatépetl and Iztaccíhuatl came to be. And even today, el Popo still smokes from the torch of that great and handsome warrior."

Vivi laughed. "I think you watch too many telenovelas, Alita." Then she turned to me and said, "Imagine if you put that down on the test, you'd get a big fat F."

"That's not the point," I said. "She's telling us these stories because we have a history that goes back to the beginning of time, right, Alita?"

"We?" Vivi said angrily, "You're not even Mexican."

"Am too," I cried. "Half Mexican. It counts."

"Lalo is right," Alita said. "Las historias y leyendas de nuestro país go back thousands of years."

"It's just a stupid myth."

"You don't get it," I said.

"What I do get"—Vivi stood and tapped the side of her head with the palm of her hand—"is that the lockdown is affecting your brains."

"Viviana," Alita said. "No seas necia. You need to know where you come from to know who you are."

"I know exactly who I am," Vivi argued. "And here's a news

flash, you're not in Mexico anymore. Your stories don't mean anything here."

"It doesn't matter where you live," Alita said calmly, but her eyes were narrow. "You're Mexican. Be proud. And you too," she said, and tapped my arm. "Pero, por el amor de Dios, work on your Spanish, ¡qué vergüenza!"

28.

A little while later, I was on my way to the storage closet when I bumped into Vivi on the stairs. We both stopped and stared at each other. I blinked twice. She blinked once. I didn't know what to say. Then she nodded. "What's up?"

"Nothing." I turned away for a moment like a reflex. When she didn't say anything, I added, "What about you?"

She shrugged and showed me the binoculars. "I was going to give these back to you?"

"You're not spying on Robachico anymore?"

"I don't know," she said, "it's not fun doing it alone."

"I know."

"Where you going?"

"Nowhere." I didn't know why I said that. Maybe it was because we were finally talking and I didn't want to mess it up by reminding her of the storage closet and everything that happened the other day. I didn't want to freak her out. But that was exactly where I was going. The old radio. I had to find out why I remembered things when I turned it on.

"So . . . ," she said. "If you want to go to the roof and, like, spy on Robachico, I might be into it. Digo, si quieres."

I smiled, but she probably couldn't tell because of my mask. "Sure. I guess."

I followed her up the stairs. Someone was playing ranchera music—Mexican songs with trumpets and guitars and a lot of yelling. Probably Sunday. He could be like Alita, get all nostalgic about the home he left behind in Mexico. But it had to have been a long time ago because Alita said Sunday had been here since he was a little boy.

When we got to the roof, Vivi stopped. Claudio and Hugo were standing in the middle of the roof—with Misty. She saw us and waved for us to come. Claudio and Hugo turned to look, saw us. Ignored us.

Vivi glanced at me.

I stepped down a couple of steps. "I'm not going."

"Misty's there," Vivi said. "Hugo can't hurt you."

Claudio and Hugo paced slowly, eyes on the ground. Misty pointed at something near Claudio's foot. Hugo leaned over, shook a can up and down a few times, then leaned in and spray-painted something on the ground.

"It's the banner," Vivi said. "They're painting the banner. We should go."

Misty pulled her mask down and called us. "Come on, kids. We're making a sign for your mothers."

Vivi looked at me, her eyes squinty and bright. I was sure she was smiling.

"It's cool," I said. "You go."

Claudio leaned over and pulled the end of the canvas to stretch it, then spray-painted something. Misty nodded and patted him on the back. Hugo stepped back from the canvas and raised his eyes, checked us out again. I couldn't tell what his deal was because of his mask, but he stared at us for a long time. Then he shook the can again, knelt by the canvas, and painted.

"It'll be fine," Vivi said.

"What about Robachico?"

"We can do that another time." She handed me the binoculars and started walking to where Misty was standing. "It's not like the motor home's going anywhere."

Hugo handed Vivi a can of spray paint and pointed at a section of the long canvas. She nodded, shook the can up and down, then crouched and sprayed. Claudio watched her work. When she finished, he nodded and pointed like he was explaining something. Hugo joined them as if suddenly they were all best friends. I couldn't tell what the canvas looked like or what it said. But Misty had said the banner was supposed to be for our moms. Hugo had nothing to do with it. I didn't see why he had to be a part of it.

29.

I went downstairs and made my way to the back of the building. Socrates's car sat in the same place with the hood up, but no Socrates—probably went to find a tool or something. I snuck into the closet real quick and closed the door behind me.

I went straight to the radio. It was strange. Every time I turned it on, I remembered something. But it was more than a memory. It felt as if I had been there in person, like it was taking me . . . to the past. Maybe Vivi was right. Maybe a memory machine was also a type of time machine. The problem was, I didn't know how it worked. Or why.

I tried to decipher how the numbers might translate into time. But there was no clock or calendar or anything that I could adjust for time. The words and numbers didn't make any sense.

I turned one of the small knobs half a turn counterclockwise, then switched the radio on. The bulbs glowed, then the faceplate flickered and slowly turned amber, orange. Then—flash.

I saw me again. I was the same age as before, but I was

standing in the apartment we live in now, holding the photograph of my father in the gold frame that now sat on the TV. The living room was empty, no furniture or anything.

A moment later Ma marched in, looking real serious. She had her hair in a braid and was wearing jeans and a T-shirt. She pointed to the side of the living room. "There, with the back against the window."

Two men came in carrying our couch. They set it where my mom told them and walked out. Ma stared at the couch. Then she saw little me and sighed. She tore the photo from my hands. "Ya, Lalo, por favor. Go to your room and unpack your things."

"But, Ma—"

"Enough!"

I peeked in the room. Claudio lay on his unmade bed staring at the wall. My bed was on the other side of the room with a bunch of boxes on it.

The men who brought the couch came back into the apartment with our dining room table. Ma was standing in the middle of the living room holding Papi's picture and staring at it.

"¿Señora?" one of the men said.

She nodded quickly and pointed to the area by the kitchen. "There."

She wiped her tears real quick with the back of her hand. But five-year-old me couldn't see that because she had her back to the bedroom door. But then Ma set Papi's photo facedown on the table the men had just brought in. And when she turned, she saw five-year-old me looking at her. She yelled, "In your room!"

Five-year-old me stepped back in the room. Claudio was

sitting up, checking him out with a deep frown. "What'd you do now, fool?"

Five-year-old me ignored him. But there was this invisible thickness that closed in on my five-year-old body, pressed against it, made it difficult to breathe. His heart raced. He gasped for air. I could feel it myself as if it were happening to me now. Claudio jumped out of bed and ran out of the room. A moment later, Ma came in with the puff-puff. She sat me down and set the mask against my face and gave me a dose from the asthma inhaler. She didn't sing the song. She just stared at her Mickey Mouse watch. Five-year-old me stared at the little brown bears, and I could feel him hating the bears, hating the inhaler, hating everything.

The weight lifted from his chest, but something else lingered inside like an echo. It was as if everything in his brain—his thoughts and memories and feelings—had been dumped out and he was left with nothing. It was exactly how I felt now in the present. It was as if something had been taken away and the emptiness it left was never filled again. Five-year-old me didn't get it. But I did. That hollowness, that anger—it was the same as when I argued with Vivi or had a fight with Claudio or when I couldn't remember something. I didn't realize it then, but that's when I stopped remembering.

It was difficult to tell which were my thoughts and feelings, and which ones belonged to five-year-old me, the Lalo in the memory. Unless maybe our feelings were one and I was really there.

Five-year-old me sat on the bed and sifted through the contents of an old shoe box. He pulled out a small pin of the Haitian flag and a small stuffed toy, a bunny with long floppy ears, and a figurine of the skeleton lady—la Catrina. It was about the size of a G.I. Joe, made of clay, and painted in bright colors. He held it up and turned it slowly, its head bobbing around while he hummed a song I didn't recognize.

When Claudio came back in the room, he tore the figurine away from him and threw it against the wall. La Catrina shattered into little pieces. Five-year-old me screamed.

"I hate you!" Claudio yelled, and stormed out of the room.

Ma called after him, but he left the apartment, slammed the door behind him. Ma came running into the bedroom. "What happened?"

Five-year-old me shrugged, avoided looking at her eyes. Instead, he stared at the floor where the pieces of la Catrina were scattered.

"Lalo . . ." Ma's whole body stooped as if someone had punched her in the stomach. She had dark circles under her eyes and the tone of her voice sounded weak, exhausted. She shook her head and turned to go. Then she stopped. She grabbed five-year-old me by the shoulders and shook him. "What is wrong with you!"

30.

It was dark when I walked out of the closet. The neighborhood was dead quiet—no music or loud TVs or people arguing or Socrates cussing up a storm from under the hood of a car he was fixing. It was as if I'd stepped into an empty world.

As I made my way up the stairs, I glanced across the parking lot. The motor home was gone.

I raced up to Vivi's apartment and knocked on the door. No one came. I knocked again, louder. Vivi had to see this. She was going to freak. The motor home. Robachico. Gone.

I knocked harder, pounded on the door with the side of my fist.

Finally, the lock clicked and the door swung open. Lupe stood with one hand on the doorknob, another on her hip. She wore a long black T-shirt. Her hair was loose, eyes puffy. She wasn't wearing a mask. "What the heck, Lalo?"

"Vivi." I stepped back. "Where's Vivi?"

"She's asleep."

"I need to see her."

"Dude, it's two in the morning. Your mom's been looking for you."

"What?"

"Go home."

I turned to look at the parking lot and up and down the walkway. All the windows were dark.

"Sorry. I . . . I didn't know . . ."

"You're loco," she said with a smirk.

"It's just that . . . the motor . . . I guess I lost track of time . . . I . . ."

She nodded and ran her hand over her hair and cracked a little smile. "You better come up with a real good excuse 'cause your mom's gonna kill you."

"I was in . . . I was . . ."

Lupe grinned and whispered, "Tell her you fell asleep somewhere."

It took me a moment to understand. She was helping me. "But where?"

"I don't know, but I'm sure you'll come up with something good." Then she winked at me and closed the door.

I walked back home but kept stealing glances at the far end of the parking lot where the motor home used to be. I couldn't believe it was gone. I told myself I had to remember this. I had to write a note on my hand as soon as I got home. And Lupe. She helped me—kind of. But even better, she said I would come up with something good. She believed in me. She said I could figure it out. I could do this. I smiled thinking about it, how she didn't treat me like a helpless child.

Claudio was standing by the kitchen counter when I walked in the door. "Where the hell you been, fool?"

"What's it to you?" I said.

"Ma!" Claudio called. "He's home."

"Lalo!" Ma ran out of her room and hugged me. Her neck smelled of soap and cream. Her hair tickled my face.

"I was worried sick," she said, still holding me tight, her fingers digging into my arms. Behind her I could see Claudio spreading peanut butter on a piece of bread, his eyes on Ma and me.

Ma loosened her grip, held my shoulders, and stared at me with her big brown eyes, dark and puffy half circles under them. She still had the marks of her mask on her cheeks. Her nose and chin had broken out with a bunch of tiny pimples. "Where were you?"

"I . . . I was . . . I fell asleep."

"Where? What's going on?"

"Nothing."

"Lalo," she said flatly. "Where were you?"

"I was just walking around." I hated lying. I never lied, especially to her. But I couldn't tell her the truth. "And I sat down and I guess I fell asleep."

"You know you're not supposed to be out on the street." Her voice was deep. I could tell she was doing her best to hold back her anger. "And at this hour, what were you thinking?"

"Too bad you can't ground him," Claudio said with a mouthful. "'Cause we're all already grounded."

Ma glared at him. "Go to your room."

"I wanna see—"

"Now!" Ma barked.

Claudio slid off the stool and walked slowly to our bedroom.

"The door!" Ma cried.

When he closed the door, I said, "I'm sorry. It's just that— I don't know. It's all just really weird."

"Weird how?" Her tone was gentle now. She caressed my head. "You know you can talk to me, Lalo. Why don't you tell me what's going on?"

A giant knot was building up in my throat, but I didn't know why. "Vivi and I got in a fight, and now she won't talk to me."

"These things happen."

"I know. And we made up, kind of. But there's something else. I think . . . I think I'm starting to remember stuff."

"You told me." She smiled and took my hands in hers. "But that's a good thing."

"I remembered when we moved here. Two men carried the couch and that table. There were boxes."

"Yes." She caressed the side of my face. "That's fantastic, Lalo."

I nodded and looked down to avoid her eyes. She seemed so excited about it. But I didn't know how to get into it, or if I even should. Just thinking about it made my stomach queasy. "Why was Claudio so angry at me? And you. You were angry, too. I was looking at the picture of Papi and you took it from me."

We both turned to look at the photograph on the TV. "I'm sorry . . . I don't know," she said. "I don't remember that."

"Remember the Catrina?"

She nodded.

"Claudio took it from me and broke it."

"Mi amor." Ma wiped my tears, her thumb moving gently over my cheeks. "It was a very difficult time for us."

"It was after Papi died, right?"

She nodded. But her eyes seemed to go far away. She was exhausted—not for now, but for always—and Papi was something she didn't like to talk about. I touched the indentation the mask had left on her face, ran my finger down the side of her cheek, tracing the red line. "Did you do the cream?"

She nodded and her eyes welled up. "I was afraid something had happened to you, mi amor. Please. Please, don't stay out like that. And don't leave the building, not during the pandemic. I would die if something ever happened to you."

"I always wear my mask, even when I'm outside."

She smiled again, her big teeth catching the light of the kitchen. "Thank you for that. I know it's uncomfortable, but we need to do it to stay safe."

"Is the lockdown ever going to be over?"

"Of course it is."

"When?"

Her eyes looked past me, as if she were staring into the future. Then she searched my face as if the answer was hiding inside me. "No one knows."

"What if Covid never goes away?"

"It will," she said, and pulled me close. "It might take a while, but it will go away. I promise."

31.

Ma went to work early the next day. She left a note on the refrigerator saying she would be back in two days and for Claudio and me to make a list of what we needed from the grocery store.

All morning Claudio kept looking at me weird as if I was hiding something. When we were in the kitchen getting breakfast, he finally spoke up. "Whatchoo up to, fool?"

Claudio had been calling me fool since forever. It always annoyed me, but for some reason, I had always dismissed it. I guess it wasn't worth the argument. It wasn't as if he was going stop, so why bother. I don't know if it was the lack of sleep or what, but this time when he said it, it really got to me—*fool*. It was such a stupid word. I hated it. "Why do you do that?"

"Do what?"

"Call me fool all the time."

"'Cause you're a fool, fool." He snorted and laughed as if it was the funniest thing in the world.

"Well, I'm not," I said seriously. "And you know that. So stop it."

He blinked, looked as if he was going to say something but didn't. He filled his glass with tap water and took a long drink, his eyes avoiding mine.

"I mean it," I said. "I hate it when you do that, so please stop."

He ignored me and pulled out a new box of Cap'n Crunch from the cabinet. "You freaked the crap out of Ma last night."

"Right," I said, "as if you're always home when you're supposed to be."

"That's different. She don't worry about me like she worries about you."

It was true. Even before the lockdown, when Claudio got home late, Ma got angry. If I was late, she worried.

I put my plate in the sink and grabbed my backpack and walked out of the apartment with a smile under my mask. Claudio didn't call me a fool again.

The motor home was in exactly the same place it had always been. It looked as if it never even moved. My first thought was that I had imagined everything. That maybe it had all been a dream—the radio, the memory, Lupe smiling at me, getting home at two in the morning, Ma getting upset. But I had a note on my hand, *motor home gone last night.* It was right there in blue ink across the back of my hand. It had to be true.

When I got to Vivi's apartment, she confirmed it was real. "Dude, your mom came by in the middle of the night looking for you."

"I know."

"Where were you?"

"Where do you think?" I said.

"She was super worried." She stared at me for a moment. She seemed afraid, or like she couldn't believe I had done something so terrible.

"You're not gonna believe me when I tell you," I said.

Whatever I experienced through the radio—the memories I witnessed—stayed with me. I didn't forget even the smallest details. And it wasn't just what happened or what I saw—it was what I felt.

"So, last night—" I started to tell Vivi, but stopped because Claudio walked in. He gave me a suspicious glance, eyes squinty and mean, but he didn't say a word.

After he passed, I leaned toward Vivi and whispered, "Last night when I walked out of the storage closet, the motor home was gone."

"Liar."

I showed her the note on my hand. "I swear."

She stood. "It's gone?"

I grabbed her arm and pulled her back to her seat. "No. It's in the same place. But it wasn't there last night."

"Weird."

"It's not abandoned," I said. "Can't be."

"We need to find out what's going on."

"Totally." This time I agreed with Vivi. The mystery of Robachico was getting creepier by the day. First the mango, now the motor home disappearing and reappearing. But as much as

I wanted to spy on Robachico, what I really wanted to do was find out what the deal was with the radio. It was helping me remember. But it was more than that. It was taking me to moments from my past like maybe it was a memory machine but also some kind of time machine. And the only way I could find out was for Vivi to try it. Or maybe she could film me with the movie camera. Then I'd know for sure what was going on.

"I have the binoculars," she said. "We should go to the roof after school."

"What about your new friends?"

She glanced at Claudio folded over his phone at the kitchen counter. "I wouldn't exactly call them friends, but they're not so bad. Hugo's pretty funny once you get his sense of humor."

"He called you a pig, remember?"

"Yeah, but now we laugh about it. Besides, we're painting a banner for our moms," she said. "You should help. It's fun."

"Yeah, I'll pass."

She tapped her cheek with her pencil. "We'll have to figure something out soon. If Robachico's on the move, he might escape."

"Or maybe he's going out at night looking for children to steal."

"Makes sense," she said seriously. "That's why the motor home's there during the day."

Alita, who had been sitting back on the couch embroidering her masks, leaned forward and spoke to the empty space in front of her. "You have it wrong, mi amor. It was chocolate chip."

She set her embroidery aside and sat at attention for a

moment, as if listening to the silence. Then she said, "Sí, claro, Danesa 33 in the neighborhood. You always got two scoops of chocolate. De eso sí te acuerdas. But I always had the chocolate chip."

I nudged Vivi with my elbow and nodded toward Alita. "She's doing it again."

"She's losing her marbles."

"I think she's talking to José."

"To his spirit."

"I wish I could see him."

32.

After school, I refused to go up on the roof while Claudio and Hugo were there, so Vivi and I stood on the walkway outside her apartment looking down at the motor home. "Maybe I didn't see what I think I saw," I said, and reread the note on my hand.

Vivi took another look with the binoculars. "Honestly, I'm sure you saw it."

"Yeah, but maybe I was wrong."

"Dude, Lupe said you knocked on our door."

"Yeah, to tell you."

"¿Entonces?" she said. "You wouldn't have come up otherwise, right?"

"I guess." My eyes were on the motor home, but my brain was thinking about the radio. It was strange that the motor home had not been there last night. But this was a waste of time. We'd been spying on the stupid thing for weeks and nothing had come of it. Meanwhile, I was dying to find out how the radio worked—and if it was really a time machine.

"Listen," I said after a long silence. "I know you're not going to believe this, but I think I went back in time."

"With the PS3?"

"No. The radio."

She put down the binoculars. "How's that even possible?"

"I don't know. That's why I need your help."

"No soy tonta," she said, and laughed. "You just want to get me down there so I can get stuck in the dryer or something."

"I need a witness. Vivi, I swear there's something going on with that thing, and the only way I can know for sure is if someone else sees it."

"Sees what?"

"If I really go back in time."

"And that someone has to be me," she said.

"You can use the movie camera and record the whole thing."

I stared into her eyes. I wanted her to see I was being honest. And that it was important for me. Because if it worked, if the radio took me back in time, I would be able to see my dad.

"I swear, Lalo. If you're pulling my leg . . ."

When we came running around to the back of the building, Vivi stopped in her tracks. "What the—"

"It's Socrates's car," I said. "It's vintage."

"Trash is more like it."

I walked into the closet, but Vivi stayed behind, holding the door open. "Maybe we shouldn't close it, just in case."

"We can't." I turned the light on. "Socrates or Nazario might see us."

She eased the door closed and came in. We stood side by side in front of the radio. I pointed to the small dial on the bottom. "When I turn it on, it flashes real bright and takes me to the past. Last night it took me back to the day we moved into our apartment here. It's like watching a movie, but you can feel what you felt in the past."

She ran her hand slowly over the surface of the glass. "How does it work?"

"I don't know. I turn it on and it just happens."

"How do you pick where you wanna go in time?"

"Yesterday, I turned this dial to the left," I said. "I thought it would make it go farther back in time. But I think it did the opposite."

"So, if you want to go into the future, you turn it all the way to the left."

"Why would you want to go to the future?"

"To see what happens with the Covid, stupid."

"Don't call me that!"

She stepped back and glanced at the door. It was closed level with the threshold so you could see a thin crack of light. "Tell me you don't want to know what's going to happen."

"Honestly, I want to know what happened in my past." I placed my hand on the switch below the dial. "You ready?"

"Wait." She got the movie camera from the case and focused on me. "Okay, go."

I turned it on. The bulbs in the back came on slowly, blue

and orange and purple dots reflecting on the glass of the picture of the ocean. The faceplate glowed a deep yellow. The speaker hissed. And that was it. Nothing happened.

"Are we there yet?"

"I don't know what's wrong." I turned another dial all the way to the left, but all we got was hiss from the speaker.

Vivi put the camera down.

I slapped the top of the radio a couple of times with the palm of my hand and turned the dials back and forth, but I got nothing.

Vivi wandered. She searched a couple of open boxes, moving whatever was inside as if she were shopping the bargain bin at the thrift store. She picked out a big book and sat on the broken microwave.

I switched the radio off and on again, checked that all the little bulbs were lighting up. Everything was the way it always was, but the dial still didn't flash—no trip to the past or future or anywhere.

I glanced over at Vivi. She turned the pages of the book, an album full of glossy black-and-white photos. The men wore suits and ties, and the women wore long dresses. Everyone looked real formal except for a few photos where the people were outside in a park. In all the pictures, they stared at the camera, smiling. You'd think that in the olden times people were always happy.

"Who do you think they are?" I said.

"Who knows." She turned the page and ran her finger over the pictures. The houses were small and plain, but the cars were big and round, older than Socrates's. "Probably someone's grandparents."

"Why would they leave them here?"

"Maybe they don't have room in their apartment," she said, and pointed at a woman standing in front of a little house. "She's pretty."

"It barely takes up any room."

"What's the big deal?"

"They're throwing away their memories," I said. "How are they gonna remember?"

"Dude, it's a storage room. This place is like a closet full of memories."

"You don't get it," I said. To me, memories were super important. I only had a few. I wanted more. I needed to know what my life had been like before now. And these people were throwing their memories away, locking them up in a closet. It wasn't fair.

"Hey!" Vivi pointed at a little boy in one of the pictures. "That's Sunday!"

He had long black hair and was wearing a white T-shirt, shorts, and sandals. "No it isn't," I said. "Sunday has a mustache."

"Are you serious?"

"Well, he does."

She tapped the photo with her finger a couple of times. "He was a kid. How could he have a mustache?"

We laughed. Then she closed the album. "Come on, let's go spy on Robachico."

"Wait a sec." I went back to the radio. "Let's try it again."

"Come on, Lalo. This is so boring."

"Five minutes. Please?"

She rolled her eyes and sat on the microwave. I flipped the switch. The bulbs turned on, the faceplate glowed, then it flashed. I saw Claudio. He was like six years old. He had his hands up trying to reach me. He was worried, almost crying. Someone was singing. A radio. Ma was dancing in the background. Laughter. Papi. He was there. I couldn't see him, but he was there. I could hear his voice, smell his cologne—feel his love.

Then I was back in the closet. I turned to Vivi. "Did you see it?"

"I saw a flash, yeah."

"I went back in time. Did you film it?"

"No." She glanced at the dryer. The camera was sitting on top of the case. "But you didn't go anywhere. You were standing right there."

"I saw Claudio when he was little. And my mom, and my—" I stopped. I didn't actually see Papi. It just felt as if he were there. Still, it felt so good—even if it was only for a few seconds.

"Yeah, if you say so." Vivi stood and started toward the door.

I grabbed her arm. "Try it," I said. "Please, Vivi. It's real. I swear."

She gave me this look, her eyes clouded with doubt. I guess I couldn't blame her. But I knew if she tried it and went back in time, she would believe me. Then I would be one hundred percent sure the radio was a real time machine. And I'd know I wasn't loco.

"Five minutes," she said, holding her hand up, her fingers spread out like a star. "Five."

She stood facing the radio and ran her fingers over the glass and tapped it a couple of times. "But I want to go to the future."

I switched it on. The bulbs glowed purple and orange. The speaker hissed. It was starting. "When the faceplate flashes," I said.

"What does this do?" She turned one of the small dials.

"Don't!" I smacked her hand.

"What the heck?"

"Don't touch anything. Just in case."

"In case of what?"

"I don't want you to mess it up," I said.

The faceplate glowed orange and yellow. I stepped away to give her room.

"What now?"

"Just wait."

She stood with her back straight, hands at her waist like a statue. "For what?"

"Shh."

A few minutes passed. She didn't move, her eyes focused on the Zenith logo like she was hypnotized. Another minute. Then she laughed.

"What?"

"That was awesome!"

"What happened?"

"I went to the future," she said, her eyes wide.

"For real?"

"There was no Covid. And we had flying cars and robots and all kinds of cool stuff."

"But . . . but— It didn't flash."

"Lalo—"

"I went to the past." I checked the dials. The long needle was in the same place where I always had it. Nothing had changed. "How come you went to the future?"

"Why don't you want to go to the future?"

"I told you. I want to learn about my past. I want . . . I want to see my dad."

"I wish . . . ," she said, "I wish I could go to the past to warn everyone about Covid before it happened."

"It doesn't work like that. You can see but you can't talk. It's like a movie but real."

"Lalo," she said seriously, her voice dropping and her eyes narrowing. "I didn't go to the future. I didn't go anywhere."

"But you said—"

"I just stood there like an idiot. There's no such thing as time travel. It's scientifically impossible."

"But it works, I swear!"

"It's just an old radio."

"But you said that when I turned my PS3 into a memory machine it would really be a time machine. You said it."

"It was just in theory." She stepped out of the closet. "Now, come on, let's spy on Robachico."

"I can't." I placed my hand on the top of the radio. Its power vibrated through me. I could feel it all over, in my bones, even in my teeth. "I need to find out what's going on."

She stared at me for a moment as if she was trying to make up her mind whether to stay or go. Then she rolled her eyes. "Fine. I'm outta here."

My hand trembled as I reached for the dial. I took a deep breath and told myself to chill. Maybe it hadn't worked for Vivi because she didn't believe in it—she didn't give it a chance. Like Alita had said, you have to open your heart to magic. Vivi refused to believe. But not me. I believed one hundred percent.

I turned the switch on. The faceplate flashed.

33.

The next day, I was a zombie. My brain was mush. I hadn't slept all night. I kept thinking of stuff. Like, if I was really going back in time, how come I couldn't see my father. I saw Ma and Claudio but not him. I was there. He was there. It was obvious. Yet, I couldn't *see* him. It was like a dreamy vision that never came together. Like at night when the room is dark and you see things, like a towel on the floor and you can't really tell what it is, and it looks like a dog sleeping or an alligator or a monster but not like a towel. It was like that but different because I didn't see him at all. And yet I knew he was there. I knew it in my heart.

I also didn't understand why Vivi refused to give the radio a chance. It was the only way I could prove it was taking me to the past. And even worse, she made fun of it—of me—saying she went to the future. We'd spent days spying on Robachico because that's what she wanted to do. We used my binoculars. I even risked my life placing the mango on his step and knocking on the door of the motor home. But she didn't want to give the time machine five stupid minutes. It was selfish. It wasn't fair.

That morning when I got to Vivi's for school, Alita brought us hot chocolate and a plate with sweet rolls. "Pan dulce from Loly's Bakery, niños," she announced real proud. "A treat for working so hard on your studies. Los felicito."

I took a concha, a roll in the shape of a seashell, with dark chocolate frosting. "Thank you."

"Gracias," Alita corrected me.

"Gracias," I said.

"De nada."

Just then Lupe stormed out of her room, marched right past us, avoiding eye contact, and went into the kitchen. She poured herself a glass of milk, went back to her room, and slammed the door, leaving the milk carton on the counter.

That was the first time I'd ever seen her come out of her room during school. I glanced at Vivi, but she was busy pulling off pieces from her sweet roll and shoving them in her mouth one after the other like a rodent.

"Esa niña," Alita said to herself, but loud enough for us to hear. She went into kitchen, put the milk back in the fridge, and went back to the couch, still talking to herself. "What am I going to do with her?"

I nudged Vivi. "What's going on?"

"What?"

"With Lupe."

"The usual." She shrugged, took a big pinch of her bread, and examined it real carefully. "She had another one of her tantrums last night. Even Sunday came by to make sure we were okay."

"Maybe she should sit out here with us."

"Right." She tossed the piece of bread in her mouth. "Good luck with that."

I couldn't turn my eyes away from the hallway that led to Lupe's bedroom. I knew how she felt. I felt the same way— alone. Even when we're with a bunch of people, we can feel as if we're by ourselves.

I thought of when we were up on the roof, the way Lupe talked, her dark brown eyes and her cheekbones—her smile— and the way she was so certain about things. When I was with her, this weird energy zapped me from the inside, made the back of my neck tingle. It was the same when I went back in time, a tingling current ran through me from head to toe.

I didn't understand how Lupe could be so nice when we were alone, but then be mean at home. I knew Alita annoyed her, but there had to be more. Maybe the lockdown was getting to her.

I made my way as if I was going to the bathroom but stopped short and turned to face Lupe's door. It was black and covered with stickers—Foo Fighters, Supreme, Guns N' Roses, Vans, The Clash, and a bunch of other stuff.

I knocked a couple of times and stole a quick glance at the living room. Vivi had her face buried in a book. I waited a few seconds and knocked again. "Lupe?"

"What?"

"You okay?"

"What do you care?"

"Look," I said, thinking of how everyone treated me, Claudio and Hugo and even Vivi. "I get it. I know how you feel."

"You don't know crap about me."

I glanced at Vivi and back at the door. "Why don't you come sit with us?"

"Get lost, Lalo."

"Lupe, it's okay. No one's gonna bother you. Promise."

She didn't answer, but I knew she was there, listening. Being alone, feeling as if everyone is against you, or doesn't understand who you are, like who you really are, is one of the worst feelings in the world. I knew because I'd been living it all my life. I didn't really know how, but I knew that helping Lupe was also helping me. I knocked again.

The door swung open. "What's your problem?"

"I just—"

"You touch my door again, I'll break your nose," she barked and slammed the door.

"Lalo," Alita said. "Ya déjala, por favor. Go sit in your place."

"Yeah." Vivi glanced up from her book. "We don't want to live through another one of her episodes."

34.

On my way home after school that day, I heard Socrates arguing down in the parking lot. He was shirtless, his skin shining with sweat and blotched with smudges of grease and dirt. He was waving his hands and calling Nazario a bunch of names, a traitor and a communist and a cheat. Hugo was there, too, standing next to his father, grinning at Socrates like an idiot. None of them were wearing masks.

"I need that piece of junk out of the alley, eso es todo."

"How you want me to make any money, eh?" Socrates complained. "I can't work here, I can't work there. I can't work anywhere."

Nazario raised his hand to stop Socrates, the same way Vivi always did. "I don't want to hear it. Sácalo de aquí—just get it out of there."

Those two were always arguing. But Ma told me one time that was what good friends did. "When you think of it," she said, "those two argue like an old married couple."

"Like Claudio and me," I'd said. "We fight because we love each other."

She smiled but didn't agree or add anything to that.

When I got home, Claudio was already in our room, lying on his bed, wearing his hoodie, legs crossed, big red-and-white Air Jordans with the laces untied. He stared at his phone like he always did, didn't look up when I came in.

"Claudio."

He scrolled through his phone, fingers moving up and down.

"Claudio!"

"What?" He didn't raise his eyes.

"Do you remember when you started high school and got in a fight?"

"Whatchoo talking about, fool?"

"In ninth grade. You said some guys called you a spic, remember? You came home with a cut on your lip and a black eye. I followed you to the bathroom while you cleaned up. Then you put a frozen bag of gandules on your eye."

He glanced up from his phone and frowned. "What're you talking about gandules?"

"Because your eye was swollen. You told me how these kids called you a spic and you decked one of them and it turned into this big fight."

He leaned his head back and grinned. "You remember that?"

"Yeah. I remember we laughed 'cause we didn't even know what spic meant."

"Except it's racist," he said. "These three rednecks were whaling on me like I was a dog—seniors, too. And they woulda kicked my ass if a bunch of Mexicans hadn't jumped in to help me. That's when I decided to be one hundred percent Mexican."

"And you dropped the Haitian part of you?"

"Nah, man. I did that way earlier, when I was telling people to stop calling me Claude. Problem was, back then I was trying to be white."

"Ma was real angry," I said.

He stared at me, his head slightly tilted. "What made you bring that up?"

"Nothing."

"Spit it out, fool."

"Nothing. For some reason I remembered you coming home with a black eye, that's all."

He grabbed his phone and started scrolling and swiping the screen. "Funny how you never remember anything," he said, "but when you do, that's what you remember. Seriously."

I lay back on the bed and stared at the ceiling with a dumb smile on my face. I knew every detail of that day, thanks to the time machine. Claudio had been wearing a Marlins T-shirt, his hair was short like a crew cut—thought he was cool. And even the bag of gandules—Goya, in the red bag—and the smell of sweat and dirt, and the sound of the neighbors' TV on some talk show where people were arguing about a paternity test. It was so clear in my head, as if it had just happened.

Claudio glanced at me over his phone. "Whatchoo smiling at, fool?"

"Nothing."

I couldn't tell him. He would just make fun of me. Or the

next thing I'd find him and Hugo down in the storage closet messing with the radio. Claudio could be cool when he wanted to. But he also had a way of ruining things—even if he was right.

Like one time last fall, when I started middle school, I told him I wanted to join the robotics team. He laughed. "Dream on, fool. You need a B average to get in." He tapped the side of his head with the palm of his hand. "Those kids are the brains of the school."

"So? I know about machines. I fix my own bike."

"Socrates helps you," he said. "Trust me. Give it up now and save yourself the rejection."

He was right. They didn't accept me.

I didn't know who came up with these stupid rules. If I could go into the past and change that, I would. I thought if someone was interested in something, they should at least get a chance to try, even if they don't have the best grades. If you're doing something you love, you'd probably be real good at it. I loved robots and inventions and stuff. That's why I was fixing the PS3. You'd think the robotics team would take someone like me, even if it was on some sort of probationary period—but no. It's all about the grades.

And people asked me why I hated school.

35.

The next day, Vivi wanted to go up to the roof and spy on Robachico. "We haven't spied on him in forever," she said. "Come on, Lalo."

"What about Hugo?"

"We finished the banner. Misty says it just needs to dry for a couple of days. You can check it out. Those guys won't be up there. Promise."

"You don't know that."

"Lalo—"

"Why don't you come with me to the time machine?"

"Dude." She rolled her eyes. "Time machines don't exist."

"How do you know?"

"Because I know," she said flatly. "And even if by some totally loco chance it was possible to invent a time machine, it certainly wouldn't be by an eleven-year-old with ADHD."

"You're a real jerk, you know that?" I bit my lip to avoid yelling at her and saying everything I really wanted to say. My hands clenched into fists. I shoved them in my pockets so she wouldn't see them and walked away.

I didn't know why I was even trying with Vivi. Everyone said Lupe was the mean one, but as far as I could tell, Vivi was worse. She could have just said no. She didn't have to make fun of it and insult me like that. She always did that. I hated her.

I ran home. I was going to prove her wrong, show her that time travel was possible, and that the radio really was a time machine. And I knew exactly how to do it. I couldn't film myself with the movie camera, but I had the PS3. If I connected the PlayStation directly to the radio, I could record the past onto the hard drive, maybe even get footage of my father. I would have the evidence I needed. I would show Vivi. I would show everyone. Ma was going to be so proud. And no one would ever say I was dumb or that I had a problem or anything. I was going to be a hero and everyone was going to want to be my friend.

But the PS3 was gone.

It wasn't on my dresser or the dining table. I checked the closet and under the bed, but I knew it wasn't going to be there even before I looked.

Claudio. It had to be.

I went up to the roof, but there was no one there—not even Vivi. I ran downstairs. The parking lot and the laundry room were deserted. I made my way to the back. Socrates's old car was still there. The hood was down, but the passenger door was open. He was sitting in the back seat. I came closer. It wasn't Socrates. It was Lupe.

"What're you doing here?"

"What does it look like?" She sat with her legs stretched out to where the front passenger seat was supposed to be.

"I don't know," I said, "nothing."

"You spying on me?" She wasn't wearing a mask. Her eyes were dark, mascara smudged down her cheeks. She'd been crying.

"No. I was just . . ." I couldn't tell her where I was going. "I was trying to find Claudio."

"Did you check the roof?" She sat up and folded her legs, rested her chin on her knees. "'Cause he isn't here."

I leaned against the car and poked my head in. "How come you won't let people be nice to you?"

"'Cause people suck. They're always getting in my business." She looked away, wrapped her arms around her legs. "That's why."

Hearing Lupe and seeing her like that, curled up into a little ball, made me realize there was a bunch of stuff going on inside her nobody knew about, not Vivi or Alita or me. I didn't get why she had to act tough all the time when I was just trying to be nice. But I guess I did the same thing. I was always defensive. But that was only because people were always making fun of me.

"You're wrong," I said. I was only now starting to understand that just because people treated me nice didn't mean they thought I was dumb. But I didn't think it was that way with Lupe. "People are nice because they care."

"Yeah, right." She tilted her head to the side. "Then how come you're not hanging out with Vivi right now?"

"We wanted to do different stuff."

She looked down and was quiet for a moment. I thought she

was thinking of something to say, but she just turned her silver bicycle chain bracelet around her wrist. She had drawn on her hands again, but this time the designs were thick and dark, bolts and wires and tubes.

"What'd you draw on your hand?" I said.

"Nothing."

"It looks like the inside of Socrates's toolbox."

She rolled her eyes, but then broke into a smile. "They're steampunk designs. I like mixing things that are old with modern ideas, like robots and flying motorcycles, using old vintage parts and new rocket-like stuff. Does that make sense?"

I nodded and glanced across the alley at the dumpsters. I was thinking of the radio. It was super old, and yet, it was a time machine—something modern. I wanted to tell her about it. I was sure she would get it. But I couldn't.

Before I could open my mouth, she said, "My dad's not coming back."

"I know, because of Covid."

She shook her head. "He's staying in Mexico and he's not coming back—ever."

"But Vivi said—"

"Vivi doesn't know a damn thing." Tears welled up in her eyes. She turned away and sniffled. "My mom told me they were going to be fine once he got back. But last night he sent me a text on WhatsApp. They're getting a divorce for sure. He said he's staying down there."

"Maybe they won't. I mean, maybe after Covid—"

"Stop it. Don't try to cheer me up." She shrugged and wiped

her tears with the heel of her hand. "People get married and get divorced and get remarried and all that. It's just . . . I wish I could be with him instead of being stuck in the apartment with my grandmother and Vivi."

"Why don't you guys like Alita?"

She turned away. "She's so strict. Everything has to be perfect all the time. And she just sits there and stares at the wall like a zombie. Sometimes I think that's what she wants us to do. Just sit there and look at the wall and let time pass. I hate that."

"She's talking to the spirits—"

"Look," she said real serious. "It's not that I don't love her, but you don't live with her. She drives me crazy sometimes."

"Is that why you threw a tantrum?"

Her eyes drilled into mine, her voice shrill. "What do you want with me?"

"What? I just— I—"

"Why are you here?" she cried. "Why are you even talking to me?"

I shook my head. "I'm sorry." It must've come from deep in my heart because my tone was softer than air. It didn't even sound like me. "I guess I know what it's like to lose a dad."

She stared at me for a long time, her eyes slowly turning kind. "People always think they know what's up with you when they have no clue what's really going on inside."

I smiled because she was describing me. "I always feel like no one can see me. Like, they see me as a little kid when I'm not."

Lupe nodded. "I like talking to you, Lalo. I admit it, okay? I don't know why but I feel I can tell you things."

"Maybe because you know I'll forget them."

She laughed. "I guess . . ."

"That's why you were upset then, because of your dad?"

She nodded and looked down. "I'm sorry I threatened to break your nose."

I shrugged. "I guess I deserved it."

"No, you didn't—you don't." She raised her eyes at me. "You're a good guy, Lalo. The rest of us don't know how to appreciate it."

"Alita does."

"That's not saying much," she said, and ran her hand over her head, brushed her hair back. "I hope I'll get to move to Mexico."

"For real?"

"If my mom lets me."

She put on her mask and stepped out of the car. I moved back, my back against the wall by the door to the storage closet to give her room. "Alita makes it sound like paradise," I said.

She tossed her hair to the side. "It is, but not in the way Alita says." She put on her mask and added, "Not everything there is nice."

She stood between the building and the car, so we stood real close to each other. Her eyes were so big and dark, and her perfume smelled like one of the stores in the mall. I wanted to hug her.

"Don't tell Vivi about the divorce, okay?"

I nodded.

That was the thing about Lupe. She made me feel right, like she saw me for who I was inside, treated me like I was older. And even though she had sharp edges, she wasn't mean. She made me feel like we were equals.

She stepped back, toward the front of the car. I said, "What would you say if I told you I had a time machine?"

She adjusted her mask. "I'd say you're loco." Then she walked away but turned real quick, her eyes squinting in a smile. "I like you, Lalo. You're real."

36.

I waited for Lupe to disappear around the corner before walking into the closet. I took off my mask and stood staring at the time machine for a long time. I couldn't get Lupe out of my head and how people had her all wrong. She wasn't this angry girl. The things that upset her were legit, like her parents divorcing. It was the same with me. People thought I had a problem that made me dumb or something. So they treated me different. They were either extra nice or they avoided me as if I were a monster. But I was just a regular person. I just couldn't remember things.

I turned the switch on the time machine. The bulbs glowed. A few seconds later the faceplate flashed, and I could see myself—five-year-old me, marching on the sidewalk with a SpongeBob backpack. The streets were deserted and clean like in a dream. All the houses were the same, white and tan, with perfect green lawns and shiny cars in the driveways, no cracks or weeds in the sidewalk.

Five-year-old me marched with quick short steps, his body leaning forward, hands curled into fists, eyes ahead. He stopped on the corner in front of a light pole that had a flyer with a picture of a cat taped to it. It was impossible to tell what the cat looked like. It was just a shape, blobs of white and black. It said: LOST CAT. GOES BY MIMI. REWARD. PLEASE CALL . . .

Five-year-old me stared at the flyer for a long time. I could feel anger bubbling inside—anger and hate and guilt.

Little me tore the flyer from the light pole, ripped it to pieces, and shoved them in the backpack. Then he started again, marching like a little soldier. I could tell he was trying hard to fight the tears. When he came to another light pole with the same flyer, he pulled it off and ripped it to pieces, shoved them in the backpack.

I blinked and was back in the closet. The triangular glass at the front reflected my face like a mirror. Tears were running down my cheeks.

That night I lay in bed wondering why time moved the way it did, like water in a river. A river runs into the ocean. But where did time go?

The more I thought about it, the less sense it made. But at the same time, I realized that whenever we remembered things, we only remembered parts. No one can remember everything, like what happened at every single moment of their lives, what things sounded like, what they smelled like. We only remember bits of moments from our past. And those moments, and how we remember them, make us who we are. My problem was that I didn't have any memories to make me who I was supposed to be.

Maybe that was why Alita wanted to teach us about Mexico. I've never been to Mexico, but after hearing all her stories, I was beginning to miss it as if I'd been there. Maybe her stories were becoming my memories. When I'm old enough I'll go. I could visit Lupe and we could go to all the cool places Alita talked about.

I closed my eyes for a moment and saw the image of the cat, the blobs of black and white. In my half sleep, I whispered her name, "Mimi."

The sound of the front door closing startled me awake. "Ma?"

"It's me, mi amor." She was in the kitchen. I heard her go to into the bathroom, come out, and close the door. I waited a while to let her decompress. Then I hopped out of bed and went to her room. She was lying in bed in her pink shorts and a tan T-shirt. She had the fan on. Her face was marked with red lines and little pimples from the mask. "N95?"

She nodded.

"You want cream?"

"No, thanks," she said. "I already put some on. But come."

I lay on the bed next to her and held her hand. Her eyes were red, like she'd been crying. Ever since Covid, she cried a lot.

"How's school?"

"Good."

She looked at me and squeezed my hand. "Really?"

"Yeah. Alita's teaching me Spanish and telling me stories about Mexico."

"What about your classes?"

"Fine, I guess."

She gave me this look like she was going to say something but then turned to face the ceiling. She took a deep breath and exhaled long and slow. Her breath smelled like toothpaste.

"Why are girls smarter than boys?" I said.

She propped herself up on her side to face me. "What makes you think that?"

"Lupe and Vivi get straight As all the time. And you and Alita know everything."

Her eyes searched my face for a moment, then she lay on her back again. "All girls are not smarter than all boys. Vivi is a smart girl. She works hard for those As. You're smart, Lalo. You just don't do your schoolwork."

"'Cause I forget."

"I know you do, mi amor. It means you have to put a little extra effort. But that doesn't mean you're not smart."

"What about Lupe?"

Ma sighed. "Lupe is smart. But she also has a . . . an independent streak."

"What does that mean?"

"She likes doing things her way."

"Like Vivi. She always wants to do things her way," I said. "It's annoying."

"Yes." Ma laughed. "But the thing with Lupe is that she's headstrong. And in life we need to be flexible. We need to have an open mind so we can learn from other people's ideas and get along with others."

"I get along with Lupe, kind of."

"Good. I'm sure she could use a friend right now."

"I think people don't understand her."

"For people to understand you," Ma said, "you have to understand yourself."

"I think she understands herself. The problem is, people don't see who she really is." I said this thinking of myself as much as I was thinking of Lupe.

"It's all part of growing up."

"What about Claudio?"

"He's going through a phase. At least I hope that's all it is."

"But is he smart?"

"Sure, he is smart." She sighed. "But Claudio's Claudio."

I laughed. It was so true. Claudio was Claudio.

She took a long breath and closed her eyes. I wanted to ask her about Mimi the cat, but her body sank deep into the bed and her grip on my hand softened.

I lay in bed next to her for a long while. She smelled so clean, of soap and cream and hospital disinfectant. I closed my eyes and tried to remember my father, but all I could see was the image of a black-and-white cat.

37.

Just as classes were wrapping up the next day, there was a loud knock on the door at Vivi's apartment. Alita glanced up from her embroidering. "Viviana. Ve a ver quién es, por favor."

Vivi went to the door. It was Sunday. And Hugo. They stood outside, a few feet away from the door, masks on their faces. Sunday took his hat off and held it against his heart. He nodded at Vivi, then glanced past her to Alita. "Con su permiso, Doña. I hope we're not disturbing."

"No hay cuidado," Alita said. "How are you, Domingo?"

"I'm well, thank you," Sunday said with a nod. "We're putting up the banner and we need Claudio's help. I hope it's not a bad time."

Before Alita had a chance to answer, Claudio packed his stuff and headed to the door. "I'm good. Class is over."

"You coming, Vivi?" Hugo said.

Vivi looked at Alita. "Can I?"

Alita nodded, and Vivi ran off with Claudio and Hugo, didn't even bother to come back to the table and close her books.

"Lalo," Sunday said, "why don't you come, too? We could use an extra hand."

I shook my head and glanced at my notebook where I was supposed to be keeping a journal about the Covid lockdown, but I had only one entry that didn't say much about anything. So much had happened and all I had to show for it were a bunch of blank pages.

"You sure?" Sunday put his hat on. "The banner honors your mother."

"I have homework. And I want to keep Alita company."

Sunday nodded and closed the door.

I glanced at Vivi's notebook. She'd left it open on one of the pages of her journal. Her entries were about me: *Lalo thinks there is a time machine in the storage closet. I wish I had his imagination.* And, *Lalo says the motor home moved but I'm not sure it's true. Not that I think he's lying but that maybe he imagined it.* And, *I think Lalo is upset because I've been hanging out with Hugo and Claudio. I like hanging out with them. Maybe Lalo's jealous.* The last entry was, *Lalo can be so annoying sometimes. I can't wait for the lockdown to be over so I can hang out with my friends.*

"Lalo." Alita startled me. "It's very nice of you to stay, but there is no need to keep me company, mijo. You should go help. It sounds like fun."

I closed the notebook and sat on the couch with her. "I wanted to ask you something." I looked at her hands; the pinkish polish was flaking off her nails. "Would you go back to Mexico, I mean, if you could?"

She tilted her head to the side and adjusted the strap of her mask. "The Mexico of my youth does not exist anymore—ya no existe."

"Yeah, but it's still Mexico."

"This is true. It will always be Mexico. But last time I visited, I realized my Mexico"—she tapped her chest with the tips of her fingers—"the one that's in here, is gone forever. José is gone. Our friends are gone. You see, my nostalgia is not just for Mexico, it is for a time. It is for my past."

"Do you ever wish you could go back in time?"

Her eyes were suddenly sad. "Unfortunately, that's not possible."

"Doesn't the Mexican magic have a way for you to go back?"

"Bueno, I suppose there is always a way," she said. "They say that when you die, you go home. But until then, you are destined to live this life. I suppose my time will come soon enough."

"No, don't say that."

"It's true. Soy una viejita—I am an old lady."

"But what if you had a time machine?"

She ran her hand along the side of my cheek. "You're a sweet boy, Lalo. No cambies, eh. I love your imagination." She stood and straightened her skirt. "Now run along. Esta viejita has to take a little siesta, que estoy muy cansada."

38.

When I stepped out of Vivi's apartment, I could hear Nazario yelling orders on the floor above. "Stretch it this way . . . Hold it tight."

Across the parking lot, the motor home sat as it always had. It seemed like it had been forever since Vivi and I decided to spy on Robachico.

"We need to tie it at the top first," Claudio said.

They were all up on the fourth floor, putting up the banner on the railing in front of Misty's apartment.

I kept thinking of Vivi's journal entries. First of all, I wasn't jealous. Why would she even think that? And the only reason it was difficult to be my friend was because she always wanted to do what she wanted and never what I wanted. And she could be mean. She never told me serious stuff like Lupe did. And when I told her things, she dismissed them—like the time machine. She didn't believe me. She wouldn't even try it. And even if it was just my imagination, there was nothing wrong with that. Even Alita said it was good to have an imagination.

"Do your side," Nazario ordered. "Hugo, Vivi, pull from your side."

Sunday said something in Spanish and Misty clapped. "It's beautiful. You did a terrific job, guys." She sounded very proud. "Your moms are going to feel so honored."

"Drop your side so it's straight," Nazario said, "and tie it up pa' que quede bien."

A moment later, Lupe walked out of the apartment. "What's going on?" She glanced up even though we couldn't see anything from here unless we leaned way out over the rail.

"They're putting up the banner for our moms," I said.

She shook her head. "As if that's going to help get rid of Covid."

"At least it will make them feel appreciated."

She leaned against the railing and looked out at the parking lot. "How come you're not up there helping?"

"I don't know," I said. "What about you?"

"Can you honestly see me participating in a group activity like that?"

I laughed. "I guess not."

"There!" Nazario called out. "That should hold."

"Let's go see how it looks," Misty said. A moment later we saw them pass on the stairwell and then appear in the parking lot below us.

They walked to the middle of the lot and looked at up the building. Vivi waved at us. Lupe waved back.

"I heard you had a big fight with your brother," Lupe said.

"Seriously?" I said. "You complain about people getting in your business but you have no problem asking me that?"

"I didn't ask. I said I heard."

"He stole my PS3."

She didn't say anything. But as usual, my mind turned in circles. "Okay, so it was his," I confessed. "He bought it at a garage sale a couple of years ago, but it never worked right. It sat under the bed forever."

"So what's the big deal?"

"I was fixing it," I said. "I was going to make a . . . a machine . . ."

"A memory machine, right?"

I didn't answer.

She raised her eyebrows but didn't say anything more and we fell into this awkward silence. A part of me wanted to tell Lupe everything. But I knew she wouldn't believe it.

"Vivi told me," she said at last. "She said you wanted to record your memories."

"Yeah, something like that."

"That would've been cool," she said. I could tell from her eyes that she was smiling, but in a good way. She wasn't making fun of me.

"I'll never know now that Claudio gave Jesse the PS3."

The group below us separated slowly, each person going their own way. In a moment, Vivi came running down the walkway, her face beaming. "Hey, the banner's awesome. Amá's gonna love it."

"I'm sure," Lupe said, and turned to me. "So, we going up to the roof or what?"

She caught me totally by surprise. But what surprised me

further was when she turned to Vivi. "You coming with, or what?"

The three of us went up. On the fourth floor, Altagracia was putting a couple of sheets to dry over the balcony.

"Altagracia, no," Vivi cried. "You're gonna mess up the banner."

"¿Qué dices, niña?" Altagracia pulled the far end of the sheet so it overlapped the banner by about a foot.

"Why don't you use the dryers downstairs?" Vivi said.

"No, mi amor," Altagracia said. "Those infernal machines are rigged. You put two dollars in them and the clothes always manage to come out wet. Por favor. Eso es una estafa. I'm not falling for Nazario's greedy scams."

We continued up to the roof. Lupe removed her mask and stretched her arms out. "It's great up here."

"That's funny," Vivi said. "I've never seen you up here."

"Lalo has."

Vivi frowned at me.

Lupe walked in a circle, her face up to the sun. "I was just telling Lalo I'm going to Mexico."

"Yeah, right." Vivi sat in the middle of the roof where the gravel still had color from the spray paint for the mural.

"I'm going to go live with Papá."

"Whatever," Vivi said, and glanced at me. "You taking Lalo with you?"

"Maybe." Lupe sat next to Vivi but looked at me. "You want to come live in Mexico?"

Vivi said, "It's nothing like Alita says it is."

"He knows," Lupe said. "But it's better than here."

Vivi rolled her eyes. We were quiet for a moment. I sat between them so we now made a little circle. It was funny how Lupe and Vivi were like me and Claudio. We fought and stuff, but deep down, we loved each other. I wondered why it happened, why if we loved each other, we argued and annoyed each other so much.

"Besides," Vivi said, "Lalo's not even Mexican."

"Half of me is. I just wish I spoke Spanish for real."

"So does Vivi," Lupe said with a grin.

Vivi shrugged and turned toward the parking lot. "Spanish is overrated. Besides, people always give you a hard time for being Mexican even if you don't speak Spanish."

"Try being half Haitian," I said, and we laughed, even Lupe. I scooted back and pulled my mask down, took in a deep breath. Vivi did the same.

"Do you speak Haitian?" Lupe asked.

"It's Creole," I said. "But I don't. I don't know anything about Haiti."

"It's funny how Alita's always giving us a hard time for not speaking Spanish."

I was sure Vivi was changing the subject because talking about Haiti meant talking about my dad. But all I kept thinking about was what Claudio had said, to forget Haiti. Papi was gone and Haiti went with him. Be one hundred percent Mexican.

"You know what's funny?" I said. "We never give her a hard time about her English."

Vivi laughed. "We should do that." She pulled at a tear in

her Converse. "Honestly, I don't see why we have to be so proud of Mexico. We're also part of the United States. Can't we be proud of both?"

"Or three countries," I said because I didn't want to erase Haiti. I didn't want to erase my father.

"Okay," Lupe said. "Say there was a war between Mexico and the US, whose side would you be on?"

"Easy," I said. "The US."

"For real?"

"Me too," Vivi said.

"I don't speak Spanish," I said. "I don't even know Mexico. I'd have to be on the US side. It's the only home I know. What about you?"

"I don't know." Lupe stood and glanced at the sky. "It would depend on what the war was about."

39.

When I got back later that afternoon, Ma wasn't home. And there was no sign of Claudio. I spread peanut butter on a slice of bread and folded it in half like a sandwich. I sat on a stool and ate while thinking about what I should say to Ma when I saw her again. The problem was that I couldn't accuse Claudio of stealing the PS3. It was his PlayStation. I also couldn't tell her about the radio. She'd freak. I could already hear her, *No, Lalo. I don't want you going in there. It's dangerous.*

But it wasn't dangerous. The radio was a real time machine. It was helping me remember. And it wasn't just the long ago past. There were a ton of things that were more recent. Like, I could remember stuff from yesterday and the day before without even trying. It was as if a door in my brain had been pushed wide open and I could see the past. For the first time, I was starting to feel normal.

When I finished eating, I went down to the storage closet. Don Frank's bike was gone. But everything else was the same. I didn't waste any time turning any of the dials on the radio.

I just switched it on and watched it warm up. It flashed and the next thing I knew, I could see five-year-old me standing in the middle of the living room of the house with the orange tile floor—alone. The house seemed huge with only a plush green couch by a big picture window. A few cardboard boxes were stacked in a corner, and there was a bunch of cooking stuff on the kitchen counter. Little me was staring at the big window behind the couch that kept flashing red and blue—made me think of Christmas. Yet, something was wrong. Little me could feel it—I could feel it. The window kept turning colors: blue, black, red, black, then blue again. The image was clear, but what was actually happening was fuzzy, like a dream.

Then Ma came into the house in a hurry, hands on her face, crying. She ran into a room, then came back out and left the house—didn't say a word. Before the door slammed shut, a black moth about the size of my hand flew in and perched on the wall of the living room near the ceiling. Five-year-old me just stared at the blue window, never even noticed the moth.

Then I was back in the closet. What I'd seen reminded me of how alone I was back then. When I was little, people were always doing things near me—never with me. It was as if the world moved around me while I stood still, stuck in the same place. And then they treated me different, like something was wrong with me. All my life I wanted to be normal, but Ma and Claudio and everyone wouldn't let me be me. Just because I didn't have memories didn't mean I was a fragile little baby.

I was confused when I walked out of the closet. I looked up at the mural hanging across the railing on the fourth floor. WE LOVE OUR HEROES! was painted in big balloon letters that seemed to glow. They were very 3D and were surrounded by all kinds of colorful flowers. I wondered if Vivi painted them. And Hugo. It sounded crazy. Hugo painting flowers. I laughed and thought of Ma. She was going to love it.

I stood there for I don't know how long, just staring at the banner. The sun had gone down. The sky was deep blue with a couple of tiny yellow stars. The air smelled of food, frying garlic and meat and beans. Sunday's door was open, the glow of his television spilling onto the walkway. Misty was standing over the railing like she always did, staring at the parking lot and the street, smoking a cigarette. I could hear Altagracia talking on the phone, laughing and saying something about the rainy season in el Cibao. I thought of Vivi and Lupe and our time up on the roof, talking and laughing like real friends. Memories. This was what remembering was like. At that moment I felt this thing in my chest—my heart or my soul or something— swelling and growing and filling me with this weird, pleasant warmth. I imagined it glowing like the little bulbs in the back of the radio. Happiness. It had to be.

It was dark when I finally got home. The moment I walked through the door, my eyes landed on the photo of Papi, the big one that's framed in gold and set on the TV. He was staring at me, smiling with one side of his mouth higher than the other.

It was as if he was greeting me, saying *hi*, or *welcome home*. It made me smile.

Ma said I looked like him, that I was just like him. For the longest time I thought she said that because I had dark skin and curly hair. But now I understood that I was like him in different ways.

At Vivi's house, they have all kinds of photos of their family in Mexico and here, plus a nice colorful picture of the Virgen and one of Jesus with the glowing red heart. We don't have any of that. We just have Papi, the young man with shiny dark skin, short kinky hair, and a sideways smile, looking at us when we come home and when we leave. I'm sure Ma put the picture there so we wouldn't forget him, so we would know that even though he wasn't with us, he was there, watching over us, making sure we're okay.

I went into Ma's room and fetched the little photo album from her bedside table. I sat on her bed and flipped through the pages—one picture per page—Ma and Papi when they were young, before Claudio and me. Ma and Papi dressed up. Ma in a fluffy pink-and-purple dress, hair up, big red-and-blue earrings. Papi in a black suit like a penguin.

I had seen the photos a million times, but I finally realized something. I was looking at their lives, at memories that did not belong to me. Even if I got my memory back, I would never really know Papi—not from before I was born.

There were photos of Claudio when he was a baby and as a toddler. There is a picture of the two of us together. He's holding my hand. We're wearing pajamas with feet and smiling up at the camera. There were bows and wrapping paper on the floor and a toy fire engine, the kind you can ride. In the background where the light of the flash fell off and it got dark, Papi stood with his arms crossed, smiling. Sitting on a chair next to him was a kitten, red eyes staring at the camera.

The front door closed. A moment later Claudio marched into the room. "Whatchoo doing in Ma's room, fool?"

"Nothing." I put the album away. "I was looking at the family pictures."

He stood at the door, staring at me, his mask down below his nose. He pulled the hood off his head and went to the living room and sat on the couch.

I followed him. Claudio never sat on the couch. It was always the kitchen, the bathroom, or his bed—not the couch. Never.

He leaned forward and rested his forearms on his knees, stared ahead at the picture of Papi, and said, "Why do you do that?"

I sat on the chair in the corner at an angle from him. "I want to remember him."

He pulled off his mask and dropped it on the coffee table. "Why? It's only gonna hurt."

"I don't know." As hard as I tried to find a reason, I couldn't. At least not a real one, one that made sense. "It's just sometimes it feels as if I don't know who he was."

He didn't say anything, just stared at the mask on the table.

"It's like . . . it feels like he wasn't really my father," I said, "as if he never existed."

His lip trembled and he took a deep breath. "You're lucky." He sniffled and turned away so I wouldn't see him cry. "Every time I think of him, I miss him. And then it pisses me off. I get angry at him, angry that he's gone, even though it wasn't his fault."

40.

The next day at lunchtime, Alita served us grilled cheese sand-wiches. "American quesadillas," she said, and placed a shaky hand on my shoulder. "I know you love my quesadillas, Lalo, but I was feeling a little out of sorts yesterday and did not get a chance to go to the store."

"This is fine, thank you."

"Gracias," she corrected me.

"Gracias." I smiled under my mask. "We can have quesa-dillas another day."

"Claro que sí, mijo." She ran her hand over my hair and made her way back to the couch. "Did you see that Don Frank is home from the hospital?"

"Is he okay?" Vivi said.

"The doctor said he needs rest," Alita said, and made her way to the couch. "It might take a few weeks, but he's going to be fine."

The good news about Don Frank was as if a dark cloud had finally moved away. Everyone was relieved. And on top of that,

I wasn't forgetting things like before. It made the school day go by in a flash. I didn't even notice classes had ended. Claudio had already left and Alita had gone to her room to rest.

Vivi closed the laptop. "So, we gonna spy on Robachico or what?"

"I don't know." I wanted to hang with Vivi, but the snippets of the past that I experienced with the time machine were like a puzzle I was starting to solve little by little. I could almost taste my entire past on the tip of my tongue. I just needed more time with the time machine.

"It'll be fun," she said. "You can use the binoculars."

"Why don't we go to the storage—"

"Not the time machine, Lalo. Really."

"I could use your help."

"No gracias." She stood and stacked her books. "I'm going to find out what the deal is with Robachico, even if I have to do it alone."

"You don't have to guilt trip me about it."

"I'm not," she barked. "But we know he's up to no good and no one is doing anything about it except me." Then she stomped into her room.

I didn't waste another second. I ran down to the storage closet. I turned the dial so the long needle was at a slight angle. I placed my finger on the switch and was about to turn the radio on when the door of the closet swung open.

"Lalo." Lupe. She walked slowly to where I was and glanced over my shoulder at the radio. "Is that it?"

I nodded and moved aside so she could see it.

"Vivi told me." She ran her hand over the front of it. "Cool." The line drawings on her skin had faded, black fingernails reflected the light of the bulb like five little stars. "What does this do?"

"I don't know yet."

"Does it really work?"

I nodded. "I'll show you."

She stepped back. I pointed to the microwave so she could sit. Then I took my place in front of the radio. I took a deep breath and glanced at her. She nodded. I smiled and switched it on. The bulbs glowed and the hissing started nice and low. A moment later the faceplate flashed, filling the room with light.

I was in the nice house with the orange floor. I was five. I was crying, like, really crying. Ma was trying to calm me down. She crouched and held me in her arms. She kept saying, "It's okay, mi amor. She'll be back. They like to wander. It's what they do. Shhh."

"No!" Little me wouldn't calm down. He was pitching a major tantrum. "I want her. I want her. Now!"

"Please, Lalo, it's going to be fine."

And there, for the first time since I started time traveling, I saw my father. He stepped out of a room. He was tall and handsome like in the photographs. He wore a bathrobe. He smiled at me. His eyes were kind. Five-year-old me might not have noticed it, but I saw it now. I saw the love, like something I could touch, a pink, reddish light. It filled the room, made me think of Alita whenever she saw José. This had to be what she saw. From my place in the time machine, I saw it. I saw it all.

Ma shook her head. "No, Claude. You don't have to."

"It's fine." He smiled at five-year-old me. "Papi to the rescue, okay." He had an accent, but not Spanish. When he said *okay*, it sounded flat without the letter sound, like when you say "or what" in Spanish—*o qué*.

And then I was back in the storage closet. Lupe was standing between me and the microwave where she'd been sitting.

"Okay," she said, her eyes wide like she'd just seen a ghost. "What just happened?"

"Did you see me?"

She touched the side of my face, wiped away a tear. "Yeah, you were there, and—"

"I went to the past." I stepped away from the machine. "I saw my dad."

"Like, right now?"

I nodded. "I was there, in our old house. And he was there."

"Dude, you're freaking me out."

"But it's true," I said. "I was five. I was crying, and he was there."

"Why were you crying?"

I looked down and thought about it for a moment. "I'm not sure."

"This is too weird."

"Did I disappear?"

"No, you were standing there like a robot. You just stared at the dial. It was buzzing and hissing and flashing. Scared the crap out of me."

"I didn't go anywhere?"

"No, you were there the whole time."

"So, how did I go back in time?"

"Maybe it's your soul." She grabbed my arm and pulled me close, looked at me real serious. "Like, your body stayed here, but your soul, the real you, went away. You know, your spirit. That's who went to the past."

"Wait . . . I think . . . yeah, that makes sense."

"'Cause I could tell you weren't all there." Lupe laughed nervously. "Like you were there, but *you* weren't really there. You know what I mean?"

"I think so."

"We should tell your mom."

"No!" I said. "They'll take it away or lock the closet."

"What if it's dangerous?"

"It's not," I said. "I've already done it a bunch of times."

We both turned to look at the radio at the same time. "You wanna try it?" I said.

"No. I don't think so."

"It's okay. It doesn't hurt or anything."

"I'm good." She stepped back and moved toward the entrance. I followed her. When she stepped out, I grabbed her hand. It was warm and soft, and for a moment she held on to mine. She glanced down at it, then at me but didn't pull away.

I said, "Thank you."

"What for?"

"For seeing it, for what you said. I didn't get it, but you're right."

"Get what?"

"How the time machine works," I said. "I don't know why I didn't think of it before."

She stared at me for a second, then she looked past me at the radio. "I gotta go."

"Lupe," I said as her hand slipped away from mine. "Don't tell anyone, not even Vivi."

41.

After Lupe left, I closed the door and went back to the time machine. Everything I had suspected was true, only I wasn't physically traveling in time. My body stayed in the storage closet. But it didn't matter. Who I was, my spirit—the one Alita always talked about—was going back in time. It made perfect sense. That was why I couldn't talk to Ma and Papi or anyone. That was why they couldn't see me. I wasn't there in person. I was there in spirit—like a ghost.

I didn't touch the dials. I wanted to go back to the same moment and see what happened. But when I turned the machine on, it took me to a different time. I was still five years old, but it was later, or maybe earlier. I couldn't tell. I was alone in my bedroom. It wasn't the one I have now that I share with Claudio. This was my own room. It was new and clean, with a bed and a dresser. Five-year-old me crawled on the floor and kept saying, "Mimi? Mimi."

He checked under the bed, crawled to where the dresser was, and peeked behind it. "Here, Mimi. Meow, meow . . . Mimi?"

It was obvious little me was worried. He sat on the rug and looked around like he was lost. The room was big and unfamiliar. A thread of fear grew and quickly turned to panic. He ran out of the room and into the kitchen, where Ma was taking plates out of boxes and stacking them on the counter next to the sink.

"What's the matter, mi amor?" Her tone was tender, but she didn't stop what she was doing. "Qué pasa?"

"I can't find her."

"She could be anywhere," she said. "It's a big house."

"What if she's lost?"

"Cats are smart. They don't get lost."

"Maybe she left. Maybe she went to where we used to live."

"Why would she want to go there?"

"I dunno. Maybe she doesn't like the new house."

"But it's a beautiful house." Ma glanced at the ceiling and made her way around the kitchen island. She picked little me up and sat him on the counter. "Dios mío, you're getting so big, Lalo. Pretty soon I won't be able to pick you up."

"Ma—"

"Don't you like having your own room and a yard?"

I could sense that five-year-old me was afraid of the room. It was unfamiliar and so big and empty. It made him feel tiny and alone. He imagined that was how the cat felt—that's why she left.

"Here." Ma set him down. "Why don't you go look in the living room, I'm sure she's somewhere around here."

Little me ran to the farthest corner of the living room.

"Mimi? Mimi, where are you?" Behind the green couch was the big window, the one that turned blue, except now it was black.

Papi came into the house carrying a big cardboard box. He set it on the ground in the space between the living room and the kitchen. He arched his back, hands at his waist. "That's the last one," he said, and walked to where Ma was, gave her a kiss on the cheek. "You happy, my love?"

"Of course." She tilted her head to the side and smiled at him with her big teeth. "But it's not just because of the new house."

"Ah no?"

"It's you."

"It's us," Papi said. "Us in a new house in a new neighborhood."

"It's going to be so good for the boys."

Papi took a deep breath, puffed his chest out. "I can breathe here."

Ma gave him a kiss and went back to pulling plates and cups out of the box. Papi turned to where little me was crawling on the floor. "And you, ti tonton, what're you doing down there?"

"Looking for Mimi," little me said. "I think she ran away."

"Ah, don't worry about Mimi. She'll be back. She knows where to get her dinner."

"We have to find her."

Even though I was there only in spirit, I could feel the desperation. Papi and Ma were saying all the right things, but they had no idea of the panic five-year-old me was going through at the moment. I wanted to reach out and comfort my little self, but I couldn't.

And then I was back in the storage closet. My legs buckled. My body felt as if it were made of liquid. I stumbled and sat on the microwave. My heart was racing, pounding hard against my chest. I was scared, worried. The cat. It was because of the cat, just like when I was little. My hands were trembling, and my eyes were moist with tears for a cat I didn't even remember.

The flyers. They made sense now. But why had I been tearing them off the poles?

When I'd calmed down, I walked out of the storage closet. It was dark out. It must have been pretty late because it was dead quiet—no cars or people or anything. I couldn't even smell cooking or hear a radio playing cumbia or salsa, no TVs glowing through the windows.

A rat scurried behind the dumpsters. One of the bulbs near the stairs was out. I glanced across the parking lot at the motor home. The door was wide open.

I walked quickly but kept my eyes on the motor home. I had to tell Vivi. She had to see this.

I turned the corner. A man grabbed my arm and pulled me close. "Does your mother know where you are?"

Robachico! He was tall and ugly and mean-looking and carried a big black plastic trash bag. I opened my mouth to scream but nothing came out. He dropped the bag and pulled me closer. He stank of trash and disinfectant. His teeth were crooked. His eyes had death written all over them.

He shook me. "Does your mother—"

I kicked him in the shin as hard as I could. His grip loosened. But when I pulled my arm away, it got caught in the cord of the ID badge that hung from his neck. He leaned down and turned to the side. I twisted my arm, jerked it back, and broke free. I ran up the stairs like a bullet to our apartment and locked the door.

42.

The next morning on our way up to Vivi's, Claudio kept asking me about last night. "Spit it out, fool."

"Nothing," I said. "I was on the roof. I fell asleep."

"You think I'm stupid?"

"I don't care," I said. "You're not the boss of me."

"Yeah?" He pulled his mask up and frowned, eyes squinting. "Wait till Ma hears about it."

I ignored him. He parked himself at the kitchen counter and stared at his phone. Alita wasn't around. There was no hot chocolate, pan dulce, churros—nothing.

I took my place next to Vivi. "What's going on?"

"Alita's not feeling well," Vivi said, and opened the laptop.

The apartment was quiet like at mass. "Guess what?" I whispered.

"Why are you whispering?"

I glanced back at Claudio. I didn't want him to hear. But he was in his own world with his earbuds in, staring at his phone. I leaned closer to Vivi. "You're not going to believe this."

"Don't tell me. You went back in time."

"No. Well, yes. But that's not it," I said, annoyed by the fact that she'd stolen my thunder. "I saw Robachico."

"Liar."

"It's true. I was in the storage closet, you know, with the time machine. And when I came out, it was super late. He was on the corner by the stairs."

She squinted at me. She was either trying to read my face to see whether I was telling the truth, or smiling under her mask. "You're such a liar."

"I swear."

"When?"

"I don't know, like midnight or something, when I walked out of—"

"How do you know it was him and not some homeless perv?"

"The door of the motor home was wide open." I took a deep breath and showed her my arm even though there was nothing to see. "He grabbed my arm, right here."

"No way!" Vivi cried.

"Seriously. I was about to go up the stairs when he popped out of nowhere and grabbed me."

"What'd you do?"

"I kicked him and ran."

"Did you tell your mom?"

"She's at the clinic," I said. "Besides, what could I tell her, that I was in the closet playing with a time machine in the middle of the night?"

Vivi stared at me, reading my eyes for a moment. Finally,

she slapped the table with the palm of her hand. "We have to go back on surveillance. Like, right away."

"Maybe we should tell Alita. So someone knows . . . just in case—"

"Please." Vivi put her hand up to stop me. "She won't believe a word. Además, she'll probably just light a candle and burn some palo santo or something. We need to keep a real close eye on him. We have to catch him in the act."

"The act of what?"

"Of stealing a child."

"We're the only kids in the building," I said.

"What about Beto and Eric? And Altagracia's baby?"

"You think we should warn them?"

"No. Not yet." She adjusted her mask. "We don't wanna start a panic in the building. We have enough with Covid. Besides, we need proof. We should get the movie camera from the closet and get him on film. Otherwise, no one will believe us."

43.

After class, Vivi went into her bedroom to put on a pair of sneakers, change shirts, and fetch the binoculars. I paced back and forth in the living room. I could hear Alita coughing in her room. I stopped by the bureau and looked at the pictures of the family. The one from Alita and José's wedding was in black and white. He was always real serious. In all the pictures José never smiled—nothing like the photos of my father where he was always smiling. Weird. Alita said they were happy. Maybe even when people don't look happy, they really are happy.

Alita coughed and was quiet for a bit, then coughed again.

Vivi came out from her bedroom. She wore a bright red guayabera shirt, the binoculars in her hand. "Ready."

"Maybe we should check on Alita," I said.

"What? No." Vivi walked past me to the door. "We're on a mission."

"But still . . ." I heard Alita say something in Spanish I didn't understand. "She doesn't sound good," I said. "What if it's Covid?"

"Don't say that!"

"But shouldn't we—"

"Lupe's taking care of her, okay? She made té de manzanilla and is rubbing Vicks on her feet and stuff. She's going to be fine."

I followed Vivi upstairs. Misty was hanging out in front of her apartment like always. She leaned over the rail and took a long drag from her cigarette, her cheeks sinking in like craters. It reminded me of Alita, how she sat in the living room staring into space in silence. I hadn't thought about it before, but they were a lot alike. It made me wonder if Misty was talking to her own spirits, maybe a husband or her parents—maybe her cats.

When Misty saw us, she smiled. "What are you munchkins up to?"

"Nothing," Vivi said.

She pointed at Vivi. "I like your shirt."

"Thanks."

"Have your moms seen the banner?"

"They haven't been home," I said.

"But don't worry," Vivi said. "They're going to love it for sure."

"Certainly they will." Misty blew a cloud of smoke. "They deserve it. And more."

We made our way past Misty. She followed us with her eyes as we turned and disappeared up the secret stairs.

When we got to the roof, Vivi paused and gave me this bewildered look. *"Munchkins?"*

I shrugged and made my way to our spot at the edge of the

roof and sat. Vivi put the binoculars to her eyes and studied the parking lot.

"Was it fun?" I said after a while.

"Was what fun?"

"Painting the mural."

She put the binoculars down and glanced at me. "Kind of. Misty can be pretty bossy."

"I can imagine."

We shared an awkward silence. Her eyes had this faraway look. I knew she had to be thinking of Alita and Covid. When she saw me looking at her, she put the binoculars against her eyes again and spied the motor home.

"I wanted to help," I said. "It's just . . . I didn't want to be around Hugo and Claudio."

"I get it." She put down the binoculars and sighed. "Please tell me you're not pulling my leg about Robachico."

"I'm not. I swear. But just because he was out last night doesn't mean he's going to be out today."

Vivi seemed to think about that for a moment. "I guess you're right."

"Maybe we should spy at night."

"Maybe he's a vampire."

"Really? You don't believe in Mexican magic, but you think Robachico's a vampire?"

She laughed, but it sounded forced. Her whole self seemed different. Even her clothes, the ripped bell-bottoms and the mismatched socks were gone. She looked . . . normal, even with the red guayabera. It was as if something in Vivi had been extinguished. She glanced at the parking lot. "I'm just saying, if he only comes out at night—"

"He's not a vampire," I said.

"Look." She pointed at the street. "It's Claudio."

Claudio, Hugo, and Jesse, to be exact. The three of them crossed the street and were at the far end of the parking lot, coming toward the building. Hugo glanced up and pointed at us. They started running.

I tapped Vivi's arm and stood. "Let's go."

"It's cool. They're not going to hurt us."

"Seriously? I'm outta here."

Vivi followed me home. I closed door and turned the bolt—just in case. Vivi knelt on the couch, elbows resting on the top of the backrest, and looked out the window with the binoculars.

"We're wasting our time," I said. "He's not gonna come out in the day."

Vivi turned and set the binoculars on the coffee table. "You're so lucky you got to see him."

"It was scary. Like, for real scary."

"I know." She jumped up off the couch. "Get the camera from the storage closet. We can meet late tonight, like at midnight or something. We can spy from the roof. You won't have to worry about Hugo and those guys. I'll make a snack. It'll be like a real stakeout. And if he comes out, we'll get him on film."

44.

After Vivi left, I went down to the storage closet, but Socrates was standing in front of his car, staring at it with his hands hanging on the sides of his waist. The car's windshield was shattered, a big orange brick right smack in the center.

He kept shaking his head, saying, "Why, why, eh? ¿Por qué?"

"I don't know," I said. I thought he was asking me. "Some people just like to destroy stuff."

He turned, looked me up and down. "Why you say that? Some vandal throw a brick on my windshield, y pa' qué, eh? What is wrong with people?"

"I don't know."

Socrates had this weird way where even when he was saying nice things, he sounded angry. But right now, he sounded angry *and* sad at the same time. It was scary, like maybe he was going to cry.

"Someone hates me," he said with a firm nod, and turned to face the car, gestured at it with both hands like he was begging. "The windshield don't matter. ¿Sabes lo que te digo, chico? It's the intention. Someone hates me. Someone hates Socrates. They did this to hurt *me*!" He tapped his chest with the palm of his hand and shook his head. "No entiendo. What did I do?"

Robachico. I had no idea if he would do something like this, but he was number one in my list of suspects. I doubted he had anything against Socrates, but he was a bad guy. He stole children. Putting a brick through someone's windshield was nothing for someone like him. I looked up. Robachico—or whoever did this—probably threw the brick from the roof. And Robachico had been roaming around here last night. It was totally possible that he did it. But no way was I going to tell Socrates.

"Muchacho." Socrates scratched the top of his head and shoved his hands in the pockets of his dirty shorts. "Listen to me. Esto no se queda así. You hear me? This ain't stayin' like this. No señor."

All I could do was nod. He stared at me for a moment. I thought he was going to start yelling again, but he just shrugged and marched to the front of the building.

I went into the closet and turned the time machine on, hoping it would take me back to where I'd been the night before.

The glass triangle flashed and I saw five-year-old me again, same big house, same moment. He was still having a tantrum because of Mimi the cat—but different.

Ma kept running her hand over her hair, brushing it away from her eyes and telling little me to relax. "Mi amor," she said tenderly, but I could tell by the tightness in her tone that she was exasperated. "She has to be around here somewhere."

"I want her," five-year-old me cried. "What if something happened to her?"

Claudio walked out of a room with a big smile on his face. "Don't worry, Lalo. Nothing bad can happen here. They have a neighborhood watch. Maybe they'll help us find Mimi."

I was finally putting together the pieces. We'd just moved into a new house. Papi bought it. That's why everyone was so happy. It was in a subdivision where all the houses were the same, the lawns were perfect, and the few cars that drove past our house moved real slow—the drivers even waved. It was going to be a whole new life for us.

But there I was, five-year-old me squatting in the middle of the living room, surrounded by empty boxes, crying like a little baby because the cat ran away.

"I want Mimi!" little me cried. His chest heaved, and his eyes grew wide every time he sucked in air. I could feel it in my lungs, too, like drowning in my own breath.

"Don't, Lalo, please," Ma pleaded with little me. She rushed to her bedroom and came back with the puff-puff and the inhaler and knelt beside me. "Here, mi amor, take it easy. Breathe."

She placed the puff-puff mask against his face and began to sing the puff-puff song. Little me took a long breath and filled his lungs with medicine. I could taste it as if I was breathing in the artificial cinnamon-like taste. It even tickled the back of my throat.

Then Papi came into the living room. He had just showered and was tying his robe at the waist.

Little me inhaled the puff-puff again. When I exhaled, it came out in sobs.

"Don't worry, Lalo." Papi slid his flip-flops on and grabbed a flashlight from one of the boxes in the kitchen. "I'm going to go find Mimi, okay?"

"Claude." Ma shook her head. "It's the middle of the night."

"It's fine. I'll be back in a few minutes." He gave Ma a wink and smiled at me. "Calm down, cheri. I am going to find Mimi now."

"Can I come?" Claudio said.

"No, thank you, Ti Claude." Papi shook his head and gave him a pat on the back. "You need to shower and get ready for bed. We have a lot of work tomorrow and we're starting very early."

After he left, five-year-old me quieted down. Ma sat with him on the couch. She wiped his tears and told him Mimi was going to be fine. She explained that cats liked to explore their surroundings. "They're naturally curious animals," she said, "that's why we love them."

A moment later, she went back to unpacking the boxes in the kitchen. Little me stood on the couch and peered out the window and waited for Papi. The houses across the street were big and dark, with the curtains drawn. The palm trees in the front yards were so still they looked as if they had been cut out of cardboard. The whole street was like a movie set, dark and still and artificial.

"He's taking a long time," five-year-old me said.

"It might take a while, mi amor. Why don't you go to bed?"

"What about Mimi?"

"Don't worry about her. When you wake up tomorrow, she'll be sleeping by your feet."

"She sleeps on my pillow."

Ma laughed. "On your pillow then. Now, come on. Go brush your teeth and I'll tuck you in."

Little me fell asleep. But it was difficult to tell how much time had passed when he woke up to the sound of knocking and opening and closing doors and people talking, all of it echoing around the empty house. He sat up disoriented—a strange empty room, the smell of paper and cardboard. He walked out to the living room.

Ma was at the door. She ordered Claudio to stay inside. Then she went outside, closing the door behind her. The window was flashing blue, then black, red, then blue. Five-year-old me went to the window. Claudio joined him and pulled the curtain back. There were three police cars in our driveway. Ma was talking to them. She stepped back, then forward like she was going to fall. One of the officers grabbed her, helped her stand. Another cop—a woman—came to her side and hugged her. Ma brought her hands to her face, leaned on the woman, and cried.

The door slammed closed. Then I saw Claudio running to where Ma was.

In a flash, I was back in the storage closet, staring at the radio. The blue light of the police cars turned the window blue. Something happened to Papi. As I stepped away from the radio, the memories came back one after another in chronological order. We'd moved into the new house, the cat disappeared, and Papi went looking for her and something happened. Something terrible. Ma was crying. The police were there.

My head was spinning, and my heart beat fast and hard against my chest. I walked out of the storage closet in a daze. It felt as if my feet weren't touching the ground and my whole body buzzed with electricity. My past was coming back. I was remembering everything. I was going to be okay.

It was dark out except for a red light flashing, just like in my memory. The side of the building and Socrates's car and the dumpsters reflected red—on and off and on and off. I ran to the front of the building.

An ambulance was parked out front. Everyone was out in their pajamas, Sunday and Yonni and Socrates and Nazario and Vivi and Lupe. Misty and Altagracia were watching from the walkway on the fourth floor.

Two paramedics in white coveralls with hoods and masks, looked like space suits, rolled a gurney onto the back of the ambulance. Everyone seemed scared. Lupe and Vivi held each other, crying and staring at the back of the ambulance.

I got to them just as the paramedics closed the back door of the ambulance. "What happened?"

"Alita . . ." Lupe sniffled and turned away. "It's Covid."

"You don't know that," Vivi cried, and looked at me. "She's sick, Lalo. Like really, really sick."

45.

The next day when Claudio and I went up to Vivi's apartment for school, we found Vivi in the kitchen making pancakes. "I just talked to my mom," she said the moment we walked in. "Alita's still in the hospital,"

"I'm outta here." Claudio made an about-face and marched out.

I joined Vivi in the kitchen. "You mean the clinic, right?" The counter was a mess with batter and dirty dishes piled in the sink.

"No. The *hospital.* The ambulance took her, remember?"

"Is she going to be okay?"

"I don't know!" she snapped, then she lowered her voice. "Lalo, Lupe was right. It's Covid."

The moment Vivi said that word—Covid—the air went out of me. Maybe it was my fault. When I heard Alita coughing in her room the other day, I immediately thought of Covid. I jinxed her.

I sucked in a breath and leaned against the counter to

hold myself up even though I wasn't dizzy. I turned away and clenched my jaw to stop my tears. I didn't have to ask for details. Alita was in the hospital—a place that was full of Covid. It was bad—real bad.

Vivi mixed the pancake batter with a wire whisk. She was hyper focused, turning it faster and faster. It reminded me of when Don Frank got Covid and she turned the pages of her book without reading a word. I placed my hand on her shoulder. I wanted to tell her it was okay, that Alita would be fine. Don Frank came back. Alita would, too. But I couldn't say anything. If I opened my mouth, I'd start crying for real.

She stopped with the whisk and dropped a blob of batter on a skillet. "How many do you want?"

I heard her, but her words didn't really register. I just stared at the blob of batter, the small bubbles building and popping. The moth. I saw a black moth. Alita had said it meant someone was going to die. But when I saw the moth, it was in the past— like six years ago. It was on the wall of the new house. It didn't count, it couldn't.

"Lalo?"

I kept seeing Alita lying alone on a bed in a small hospital room, tubes connected to different parts of her body. I had asthma. I knew what it was like to have a big weight pressing against your chest, the struggle to suck in just a tiny bit of air like you're choking. It was exhausting. It was the worst feeling in the world, like drowning without water.

Vivi set a plate of pancakes for me on the counter. I stared at it not even thinking or knowing what it was. "I . . . I can't."

My stomach felt queasy. I jinxed Alita. I saw the moth. It was my fault.

Vivi stared at me, her eyes as lost as mine and red with tears. "I know," she said, her voice cracking.

I stepped away from her. I couldn't even look at the kitchen without thinking of Alita cooking for us, always so happy.

Vivi took the pan off the burner and followed me to the dining room. "At least my amá's there." She spoke real slow, as if each word was a major effort. "But since it's Covid, she hardly gets a couple of minutes with her."

We sat at the table. "I don't get it," I said. "She was always so careful. She always wore a mask."

"I know. But she would go to the store and to church and the Guadalupe Center."

"And Claudio and them—" I clenched my fists. "They go around without masks all the time."

Vivi dropped her head in her hands and wept. "I wish there was something we could do."

At last it came out of me. I'd been fighting so hard to hold it in, trying to be mature, trying to be older, but I couldn't. It came out like a storm, tears and sobs I couldn't control. "I don't want her to die."

"I wish . . ." Vivi sniffled. "I wish I had paid more attention to her stories. And that . . . and that I hadn't been so mean to her."

"You weren't mean."

"I was too!" she cried, her cheeks red and wet with tears. Her mask had slipped down to her chin. Her mouth was twisted, her eyes squinting. "I was more interested in spying on Robachico than learning about Mexican magic and all that. And I wasn't nice about it. I was a jerk."

"It's okay," I said. "She's going to be okay." I meant it for her but also for me and for Alita.

I glanced across the room at the pictures and the candles. I thought of her ancestors and José Antonio and the Mexico of her youth and the stories of the people of her pueblo. I believed everything Alita told me—Tlaloc, the rain god, and the moth and the Day of the Dead, when our dead relatives came to visit. All the magic of Mexico and the Aztecs and how it was part of what made life special for us. Our past made us whole. That's how we're able to live with so much pain, with sadness and loneliness and all those moments when we suffer for the people we love. I didn't know how much of it I believed at first. I just loved sitting with her, listening to her voice, letting her stories take me away from my own loneliness. But I did believe. I had to. If I didn't believe in spirits, I couldn't have traveled to the past and seen my father. If I didn't believe, there'd be no time machine— the time machine!

I jumped to my feet. "I'm going to help her."

"Dude"—Vivi looked at me like I was crazy—"they won't even let my mom—"

"That's not it." I raced out of the apartment and ran downstairs. If I could go back in time to when she was going to church or the store, I could warn her. I could tell her not to go, that she would get Covid. When I went back in time, I couldn't speak because I was a spirit. But Alita could hear José. And he was a spirit. If she could see and hear José, she would be able to hear me.

Just as I reached the ground floor, Socrates grabbed my arm. "Oye, chico, where you running to, eh?"

"To, uh, to—" I couldn't tell him. He wouldn't believe me. "To help Alita."

"I hear you and your friends been going up on the roof, eh?" He gripped my arm harder than Robachico and shook me like a rag doll. "Tú y la malcriada de Lupe."

"What?"

"I know her. She's bad news, always go around angry at everyone. You drop that brick on my car."

"What? No. It wasn't me. It wasn't her. I swear."

"You keep coming around all the time, you checkin' my car all the time, eh?" He was dirty with sweat and grease, no mask. The wrinkles in his face transformed him into a devil. "I know Lupe is always up to no good. And you—"

"No, I'm not." I kept pulling away. "I swear. Let me go."

"I'm gonna turn you in to the police, tell your mamá what you do, eh? You gonna pay for what you done."

"It wasn't me. Please!" He was too strong, his fingers sinking into my arm.

"I know it was you. Or Lupe. Or the other—Viviana!"

"It wasn't us," I cried. "Claudio and Hugo and that other kid Jesse go up there all the time, too. Maybe it was one of them."

His grip loosened. I tore my arm away and ran home as fast as I could.

46.

When I got home, Claudio was in the kitchen making a batido. The noise of the blender drowned out my words when I said I needed to talk to him. My heart was racing from my encounter with Socrates. And because of Alita. And all the moments from the past—my father, Mimi, the old house. They all crashed together like when you wake up from a bad dream—but then you notice it wasn't a dream and everything's messed up for real.

Claudio finally turned the blender off and poured himself the shake. "You should be in school, fool."

"So should you."

He drank, draining the glass.

"Did you and Hugo throw a brick at Socrates's car?"

"Whatchoo talking about?"

"Someone threw a brick at Socrates's car and broke the windshield. It was you guys, wasn't it?"

"You trippin', fool."

"I'm serious." I was so angry, I wanted to jump on him, let my fists fly. But I knew it was a losing battle.

"So am I." He let out a long burp and tapped his chest. "Maybe it was crazy Lupe.

"Yeah, right."

"She seems like the type who would do something like that."

"What about Hugo?"

"What about him?" he said, and walked into the bedroom.

I sat at the counter and drank what was left of the batido directly from the blender. As I sat there, letting everything sink in, I realized I wasn't angry at Socrates or Hugo and Claudio. I was angry at myself. The whole time I thought that if I knew my past, if I remembered things, things would be different. I thought I'd understand why things were the way they were, I'd have friends, I'd be happier. The time machine showed me my past, but nothing changed. I was still the same Lalo. I was still angry and confused—something was missing.

I went to the bedroom. Claudio was lying on the bed with his earbuds in. "Claudio?"

He turned on his side, away from me.

I kicked his bed. "Claudio."

"I said I didn't do it, fool."

"What happened to Papi?" I said.

He pulled one of his earbuds out and looked at me. "You know what happened."

"Tell me."

"He died."

"Yeah, but how? What happened that night?"

He sat up and pulled the other earbud out. His eyes were dark and sleepy. I was afraid he was going to lie. Ma once told me that when we lie over and over we start to believe the lie and start thinking it's the truth. Sometimes I felt that was Claudio, that he believed everything that came out of his mouth—even if it was a lie.

He bit his lower lip and turned away for a second. "Every time I tell you, you forget. Ma tells you, and you forget."

"Just tell me. Please."

"You forget. But we don't. Ma and I don't forget. We can't. And when we tell you, it's like it happens all over again. And it hurts"—he tapped his chest with the side of his fist—"in here. It hurts like hell."

"Please?" Claudio was always mad at me, but now he was different, emotional. "I'm starting to remember. Papi went out to look for Mimi, right?"

We shared a long silence. It was as if all the years were catching up to us. Time moving at the speed of light, but still stretching forever.

Claudio's lip trembled. He turned to the side and stared at the wall for a moment. When he turned back to me, a thin tear escaped the side of his eye and ran slowly down his cheek. "I don't even know why we moved to that stupid house."

"I thought he liked it."

He wiped his tears with the back of his hand and locked eyes with me. For the first time since I don't know when, we connected. We were brothers—like, real brothers. I could see in his eyes that he hated that I didn't know. That I didn't carry what he carried. That we didn't share this truth. That we didn't share this pain. Maybe that's why he was angry at me all the time.

Knowing the past was killing him as much as it was killing me not knowing.

"He got shot."

Three words, three bullets: He. Got. Shot.

I sat on the edge of my bed. "What? Why—who?"

Everything I'd seen in the time machine came back to me in the blink of an eye. All the snippets, the memories, the stories, the pictures—everything connected like one of those connect-the-dots puzzles in a coloring book.

"It was late," Claudio went on, his eyes staring down at his fingers fidgeting with the earbuds, tears streaming down his cheeks. "We'd just moved in that day. That same day."

"My cat."

"Our cat." He nodded. "I guess she got out and Papi went searching for her."

"Because I was having a tantrum, right?"

He nodded. "He never came back."

"Who— Who shot him?"

"One of the neighbors."

"Why?"

Claudio dropped his head.

"Did he go to jail?"

He raised his head and looked at me, and I could see the pain of the memory but also the relief of unburdening himself of it as he shook his head. "He was one of the neighborhood watch guys."

47.

It was my fault. Claudio didn't have to say it. I knew. I'd made such an annoying fuss about the cat, Papi had to go out and look for it. He did it for me, to make me feel better.

Claudio put in his earbuds and turned over to face the wall.

I had that strange feeling as if I were floating again, as if I were here but not here. I saw myself from somewhere else, somewhere above, a lot like when I went to the past in the time machine, except I knew it was me today—now. I walked quietly out of the apartment and went downstairs. I had to do something. I had to fix things. Maybe it was too late for Papi, but not for Alita.

I came around the building. Socrates's car was gone. The light in the storage closet was on. I ran inside. Everything had been moved around. The microwave was on the other side of the room. Boxes were open, books and papers were strewn all over the place.

The radio was turned around, shoved against the wall. I moved it, turned the dial so the long needle pointed to the bottom, trying to estimate a time in the recent past before Alita got Covid. I turned the switch, but nothing happened. I checked to see if it was connected and saw the back of the radio. The little bulbs were gone. Every. Single. One.

I looked around the closet, checked in the boxes, in the microwave. But I knew I wasn't going to find them. Someone had been here. They went through everything, moved things around. They took the bulbs. Without them there was no time machine.

I ran outside and stood in the alley where Socrates's car used to be. Someone had spray-painted the phrase THE WORLD IS TURNING on one of the dumpsters.

There was a loud pop behind me. Then another. I turned— bits of glass on the ground. Then a bulb exploded against the pavement, shattering into tiny pieces. I looked up—Hugo.

He was standing on the edge of the roof, staring down at me with a stupid grin on his ugly face. He tossed another bulb. I stepped back and covered my head with my arms. The bulb crashed by my feet and shattered. I looked up again. He waved.

"Stop it!" I cried.

He threw another bulb. It shattered behind me. I ran. I raced up the stairs as fast as I could. I was going to push that monster off the roof, finish him once and for all.

Just as I got to the fourth floor, Hugo was walking out from the secret stairs. He stopped, stood there at the end of the walk-way by Misty's apartment, his hoodie on. No mask.

"You." It came out of me in a whisper.

Then Vivi appeared from the secret stairs, no mask, the

movie camera in her hand. "Dude, you didn't wait for—" She saw me and stopped.

"Vivi . . ." My voice broke.

She stood by Hugo's side, stared at me, a blank expression on her face.

"Where you going?" Hugo was calm, not mean or angry or anything.

"You!" I spat it out. "You took the bulbs from the radio."

"Vacuum tubes." Hugo grinned. "Pretty cool how they explode, huh?"

"You broke it. You ruined everything!"

"Yeah, whatever."

"Why?" I cried. "Why would you do that?"

"It was fun."

I looked at Vivi. "You . . . You told him."

She shrugged. "It's not like was yours or anything."

"Yeah," Hugo sneered. "It's my pop's stuff. I can do what I want with it."

"But—it was my time machine. I saw my dad. I know what happened. I saw it!"

Vivi's lips moved like she was going to say something, but she didn't.

"You don't get it." I was surprisingly calm. All the anger had been spent out of me. At that moment, all the stuff that had been pressing against my chest for I don't know how long lifted away. I wasn't me anymore—not the old me, not Lalo from school, the one with accommodations, Lalo with the ADHD, Lalo with the memory problem. It was different. I remembered now. I remembered everything.

"I was going to use the time machine to help Alita," I said. "I was going to go back in time and warn her."

"No seas menso." Hugo laughed. "You can't go back in time."

"Not anymore," I said. "You broke the time machine."

Vivi's eyes grew big, then small. Her face twisted. I thought she was going to cry or scream. Hugo shoved his hands into the pockets of his hoodie and nudged her with his elbow. "Vámonos."

But Vivi didn't move. She just stood there, staring at me like I was a ghost, her eyes half squinting, her mouth moving with no sound. "You can't help her," she said at last, her voice shattering into a million pieces like the little bulbs. "Alita's dead."

48.

I couldn't move. My whole body felt as if it'd been zapped, paralyzing me in time, stuck in the place where the walkway met the stairs. My eyes fixed like lasers at the place where Hugo and Vivi had been standing—a place that no longer existed.

At that moment something left me—my mind or spirit or whatever—it floated away. I could see myself from way up, way above the roof. And what I saw below was so small, it seemed everything that had surrounded my life until that moment didn't matter. In a flash, just like the ones I experienced when I was in the time machine, I saw Alita. I saw Mexico. I tasted the bitterness of hot chocolate, the sweetness of churros, and the sweet rolls she used to give us. I felt her hand petting my knee like she did when I sat beside her on the couch and she told me about all the magic of Mexico. I wasn't trying to remember. I just did. It was automatic, like water flowing in a river. Every detail passed through me—her smell like soap and Nivea cream, the soft sound of her voice, the funny way she pronounced English words. I was so deep in the moment that I never noticed Hugo and Vivi brushing past me on their way downstairs.

I don't know how long I stood there remembering, seeing the past as if it were the present. I heard a raspy voice call my name again and again. I blinked. In a moment, I was back on the walkway.

"Lalo, you okay?" Misty stood a few feet away from me, her thin body bending toward me, no mask on her face.

"I'm sorry," I whispered.

"I beg your pardon?"

I had no idea why I'd said that, what I meant. Maybe I was speaking to Alita. Or maybe I was saying it to myself because something inside told me I needed to forgive myself.

"You look a little off," Misty said. "You all right, kiddo?"

I nodded and glanced out at the parking lot. The motor home was parked in the same place where it always was. And yet, it seemed miles away. Across the street a homeless man pushed a shopping cart. He wore a black cowboy hat and boots—made me think of Sunday.

Misty said something I didn't catch, then walked back into her apartment. Vivi's words echoed in my head—Alita is dead. Alita. Is. Dead. Alita—but there was something else. Papi.

It was my fault. He died because of me. I didn't just remember. I understood. Papi went looking for my cat that night and someone shot him because they thought he was a burglar in our new neighborhood—the clean, safe neighborhood he was so proud of.

Something strange and ugly rose from my stomach to my chest, pressed against my heart and squeezed so hard I had to clutch my chest with both hands.

I was suffocating just like when I was little and had an asthma attack. It kept pressing and pressing and wouldn't let go. I made my way slowly along the walkway and up the secret stairs to the roof. I needed space, air. I pulled off my mask and gasped. I breathed in deep, then exhaled in short, uncontrollable sobs.

The sky was blue and clean, no clouds except for a white line trailing behind an airplane. I sucked in all the air I could, gobbled it up like it was food. I thought of heaven and whether it existed and whether Papi was there. And Alita. And if it was true about our spirits. And if it was, why couldn't I see them?

I walked to the edge of the roof where I used to sit with Vivi and spy on Robachico. It seemed as if it had been ages ago. Now she was hanging out with Hugo. Alita was dead. Everything I loved had been taken away from me.

I wanted to go back in time. But Hugo was right. Time travel was impossible. And somehow, I knew that. I knew it now. And maybe I knew it then. Maybe there never was a time machine.

I could see Socrates below in the parking lot, his legs sticking out from under a car.

"Lalo!" Lupe came running from the secret stairs.

"What?"

"No!" She ran toward me. "Don't jump."

I looked down again. Socrates's hand reached out from under

the car hunting for a tool. He grabbed a pair of pliers and his hand disappeared under the car again.

I turned to Lupe. "I wasn't—"

She reached for me. I stepped to the side but my foot slipped off the edge. I lost my footing and fell back.

Lupe grabbed my arm and yanked me in. I flew forward. Our bodies crashed against each other. She held me in a hug. Our eyes locked.

When she let go of me, I took a step to the side to get a little distance from her and from the edge of the roof—just in case.

"I wasn't gonna jump," I cried and put on my mask.

"Vivi said you might because Alita—"

"Vivi? Vivi doesn't know how I feel," I said. Then I blurted out: "You do."

Lupe froze for a moment. "I have no idea what you're talking about." She turned away quickly and curled a strand of hair behind her ear. "I was just . . . scared. I really thought you were gonna do it."

"Why would I do that?"

She waved at the edge of the building where I'd been standing. "I dunno. Vivi said you were all weirded out when she told you about Alita. And when I saw you standing there, looking down, I was like, dude . . ."

I got it, though. I wasn't alone. I knew that now. I could tell she missed Alita, and her father and her mom and normal life.

"Holy crap," she said, laughing. "I almost pushed you off."

"No. You saved me."

She looked at me, no smile, no laughter, just her big brown eyes surrounded with black eyeliner staring at me in a way that told me how much she cared. I thought maybe she saw the same in me. At least I hoped she did. We all held on to things, blamed ourselves for things we couldn't control, and felt alone in our grief. But it didn't have to be that way. We saved each other.

49.

That night I sat on Ma's bed and massaged cream on her face. She kept her eyes closed. Her expression was empty, as if happiness and sadness didn't exist. I kept thinking of something Lupe had said when we were up on the roof. That Alita had finally gone home. That the magic would take her to the place where she would finally be happy, a place without nostalgia. "She's back in her Mexico, the one she loved, with her husband and everyone," Lupe had said.

My fingers traced the marks the mask made on Ma's face. I imagined they were a path to the place where Alita was going. Like the time machine that wasn't really a time machine or a memory machine. A magic path that takes us where we need to go without really knowing that's where we have to go. To where we can remember what we never really forgot. I honestly wanted to believe the radio was a memory machine or a time machine, so it took me to my past. It showed me my memories—memories that had never left me. Maybe it was going to be the same with

Alita. Her spirit, or her soul or whatever, would travel to the place she needed to go.

"Ma," I said. "Can we put out an ofrenda on the Day of the Dead?"

"Sure," she said.

"I want to make one for Papi so his spirit will know and he'll come. Alita said you don't have to be Mexican to do it."

She nodded.

"I also want to make one for Alita."

Ma opened her eyes. They welled up as she stared at me. I knew she was sad, thinking of Papi and Alita and Covid and the lockdown and how difficult everything had become for her and for everyone.

"I know she's happy wherever she's going," I said. "And if we set up a nice ofrenda on the Day of the Dead, her spirit might come visit."

"That would be nice," Ma said. "Doña Cecilia had a big heart. She lived a very difficult life, but she was never bitter about it."

"We'll need to get Cempasúchil flowers and the special bread and sugar skulls and all that stuff from the Mexican market where Alita used to shop."

Ma kept staring at me. She didn't say anything for a long time. I kept running my fingers around the lines the mask had left on her face, trying to ignore how she stared, as if she was trying to find out something I might be hiding from her.

Finally, I said, "Did you like the banner?"

She smiled. "It's beautiful. Thank you."

"I didn't work on it."

"That's okay," she said. "You take good care of me, Lalo. You put cream on my face and make me feel better. Sometimes," she said after a moment, "I see so much of your father in you."

I ran my fingers one on each side of her face so they met at the tip of her chin, almost making the shape of a heart. "I remember he went out to find for Mimi," I said. "We'd just moved into the new house, right?"

Ma blinked and sat up and turned to face me, stared at me like she was looking at a ghost.

"It was late," I went on. "But still he put on a robe and said he'd be back soon, but he never came back."

Her eyes grew wide and her lip trembled. "You remember."

"The police came to the house, and you went out. But no one told me anything."

She nodded and looked down for a moment. When she glanced up, the tears were too much for her eyes. They ran down her cheeks like two shiny lines.

"Ma . . ."

"A man shot him," she whispered slowly, her mouth tight as if she were trying to stop herself from screaming. "Three blocks from our home. They said they thought— They thought he was a burglar."

"But why, Ma? Why would they think that?"

She shook her head and pulled me close, held me tighter than she'd ever held me. But she didn't have to tell me why. I knew. He was shot because of who we were. People like us weren't supposed to live in a nice neighborhood like that.

50.

The next day I knocked on Sunday's door. He looked tired, but happy to see me. "Qué sorpresa, muchacho. How are you?"

"Good," I said. "I was wondering if you still had any mangoes?"

"Sí, como no," he said, surprised. "How many would you like?"

"Just one."

"You sure? Tengo hartos."

"Solo uno, por favor," I said, thinking of what Alita had said about learning Spanish, and how it was important to know it and to know our culture. Sunday smiled. I could tell he was proud to hear me speak Spanish, as if he also knew the language was the secret of who we really were. Alita had said that, too. "It's our culture," she'd said one afternoon after class. "It's our responsibility to know our past and use our language and pass it on to our children. That is the one thing they cannot take away from us."

Sunday went back into his apartment and came back with a

big yellow-and-red mango. "This one's nice and ripe. You sure you don't want more?"

"No, muchas gracias, Domingo."

"Bueno, don't let it sit for long or it'll go bad."

I went up to Vivi's apartment with the mango. She opened the door and just stood still, her eyes moving from me to the mango and back.

"You still dare me to knock on Robachico's door?" I said.

Her eyes grew narrow. I could tell she was smiling behind her mask. "We writing a note on it?"

"No, come on."

"Let me get the movie camera," she said, and then stopped. "Ah, never mind."

"No, get it."

"It doesn't have any film," she said, and her eyes squinted in a smile. "I guess I kind of knew that all along. Loco, huh?"

We went downstairs to the parking lot. Socrates was tinkering under the hood of another car, cursing in Spanish and talking to himself like he always did. A radio was playing one of those old Cuban songs with a lot of drums and guitar. I couldn't tell if I'd heard the song before, but it reminded me of when I used to dance with Papi. He'd pick me up and hold me in his arms while he danced around, both of us laughing like a couple of locos.

"Lalo." Vivi stopped in the middle of the parking lot. We were about fifteen yards from Robachico's motor home. "I'm sorry about your time machine. I was upset. I read your journal for class. You— You didn't write anything. And I thought— I thought you didn't care about me and that you didn't want to be friends."

"It's okay," I said.

"But still. It was selfish—"

"Hey!"

We turned at the same time. Lupe was on the walkway in front of their apartment, waving at us.

"What's her deal?" Vivi said.

I waved for Lupe to come. She waved back and ran to the stairs.

"We did all this stuff together," Vivi continued, "and you didn't write a word about it. I felt like the time machine had stolen my best friend."

She couldn't see me smile because of the mask. "I forgot about the assignment. That's why I didn't write anything."

"What?"

Lupe came running across the parking lot. "What're you guys doing?"

I showed her the mango. "We're taking it to the guy who lives in the motor home."

"Robachico," Vivi said.

"He could be anyone," I said. "Honestly we don't—"

"Dude." Vivi put up her palm like she always did. "You know exactly who we're dealing with."

But we didn't, really. We had been afraid of Robachico be-cause we didn't know him, just because of what Claudio had said. We turned him into a monster. But we didn't even know him. I didn't want to be like that.

"Come on," I said.

"Are you sure about this?" Vivi said when we reached the door of the motor home.

"Totally."

Lupe looked at us weird, like we were loco.

I knocked on the door, but no one came.

I knocked a little louder. We heard a noise inside. Vivi glanced at me and stepped back, just behind Lupe and me. The latch on the door turned and the door swung open. The man I'd seen that night stood with one hand on the door, the other adjusting the strap of an N95 mask behind his ear.

"Hello," he said. He was tall and had long messy hair, and his eyes were big and gray. But he wasn't a monster.

"Hi . . ." It came out so soft I had to cough and clear my throat and start again. "Hi. We brought you a mango."

He looked at the mango. The thin lines of crow's-feet at the ends of his eyes became more pronounced. I knew he was smiling. "Well, thank you very much. I love mangoes."

"We love them, too," Vivi said. "My grandma used to put lime and Tajín on them for us."

"I'll have to try that," the man said. He kept one hand on the door and held the mango with the other. An ID badge hung from his neck. It had his picture on it, just like Ma's, except his said CAPE CORAL HOSPITAL. When no one said anything more, he moved to go back inside.

"Sir," I said quickly, "what's your name?"

His eyes moved from me to Vivi, to Lupe, and back to me. "Randolph. Randolph Clark. My friends call me Randy."

"I'm Lalo," I said. "It's short for Eduardo. And this is Vivi and Lupe. We're friends."

ACKNOWLEDGMENTS

First and foremost, I would like to thank my wife, Lorraine, for her support and patience. I'm not always easy to be around when I'm trying to find my way into a novel and the characters take over my life. I would also like to thank my editor, Andrew Karre, whose magic with this manuscript was invaluable and for caring about my characters as much as I do. And of course, my agent, Isabelle Bleecker, for always being there for me and putting up with my moments of inspiration and desperation. And to Richy Sanchez Ayala, thank you for the awesome cover!